SLOW BURN

An Anthology of
HOUSEHOLD HORROR

A COLLECTION OF STORIES BY

Shannon Lewis · Georgina Pearsall · Harry Menear
Amber Donovan-Stevens · Kathryn Leigh

COMPILED BY

Shannon Lewis

ILLUSTRATED BY

Amber Donovan-Stevens

In association with Slow Burn Horror
slowburnhorror.com

Horror gives us a perspective on so-called common sense. It helps us see that a notion of everyday life completely secure against threats cannot be possible, and that the security of common sense is a persistent illusion.

Philip J. Nickel

Horror and the Idea of Everyday Life:
on Skeptical Threats in Psycho and The Birds

You feverishly take the chair, place it against that door without a lock, push the bed towards the door until it's stuck, and you throw yourself upon it, exhausted and yielding, with your eyes shut, and your arms clasped around your pillow: the pillow that isn't yours; nothing is yours...

Carlos Fuentes

Aura

TABLE OF CONTENTS

Preface

Shannon Lewis and
Amber Donovan-Stevens

SHANNON: IN 2019, I WAS A FRESH COLLEGE graduate, unemployed and throwing my CV at any job posting with a pulse. One afternoon I was sat in my room, rewriting my experience giving campus tours as "customer-facing engagements with an informational element" when my roommate ran up to his bedroom and emerged with a carton of eggs. I stared at him, bemused, and asked why he kept eggs in his bedroom. He shrugged, said he forgot them from when he went to the shop earlier. That was that. But I couldn't stop thinking about it. Why did it feel *so wrong* to think that he kept eggs in the bedroom? Why did it feel like he was breaking a rule?

AMBER: Shannon and I first met working on a student arts-and-literature magazine, *Octarine*, which we worked on throughout all three years of university. Ever since we graduated, we wanted to keep working together on a project. When Shannon approached me with a horror short story about eggs, we realized we had the perfect opportunity. Let's take all our post-graduation anxieties and whack them in horror stories.

SHANNON: It didn't take long for Harry, Kathryn, and Georgie, all of whom worked with us on *Octarine*, to sign on. We wrote little-to-no horror throughout our creative writing degrees, and yet it seemed like the perfect common ground for all of us. After all, we were at this stage in our lives where nothing seemed certain, either working jobs we hated or trawling job boards to find a job we could one day come to hate. Adult life outside of the comfortable bubble of university was coming at us hard. Student loans, taxes, income, saving for retirement, setting an alarm for 6 AM—these all became new realities we'd not had to experience in their entirety. So, we decided to write some stories about it.

AMBER: We were on track to publish for October 2020, right in time for Halloween, when... well you know, real-life horror happened. While the global pandemic was a crap time to launch a project, it was prime for gaining more experience into what it means to be isolated and terrified at home, questioning your sanity more with every fresh brick of homemade banana bread. In the meantime, we shifted our focus a little. We had all this creative energy and we were starved for a connection (Shannon and I were also on opposite sides of the planet at the time) so we thought: hey, the internet is a thing.

We put the anthology on the backburner (pun intended) and focused on creating something a little more fluid that could fit with our fluctuating moods during lockdown: slowburnhorror.com, a hearthstone for fans of slow burn horror. Shannon still got to write all about horror, and I got to make spooky art, and it gave us an excuse to chat every week no matter what.

SHANNON: But then it was 2023 and we had built up a good collection of blog posts exploring slow burn horror, and we decided it was time to come back to our original project. So, here we are, three years late, but better late than never. We're still in time for Halloween at least. (A/N: at the time of writing this, we were)

SHANNON: I suppose if we're writing an intro, we should probably explain exactly what we mean by slow burn horror. In a nutshell, slow burn horror is the kind of horror that drip-feeds you information. The pacing is glacial, the setup atmospheric. The overarching feeling of the stories in this anthology is that of creeping dread. It starts as that squiggly feeling in your stomach when the roller coaster first shifts onto the track, the tightness in your chest as you try to remember if you turned the oven off before you left the house. It's like being the proverbial frog in a pot of boiling water—by the time you realise the danger, it's too late.

AMBER: For the design of the anthology, Shannon and

I were drawn to the style of old encyclopaedias. There is something ornate and a little eerie about them; at one time in history, an encyclopaedia was all-knowing, a collection of immutable truths. There is, then, an inherent tension between the style and the subject: an encyclopaedia contains all the answers in the world, yet slow burn horror only yields more questions. By having a diagram at the start of each story, we provide the reader with tangible and accurate imagery that offers a sharp contrast the growing ambiguity of their reading.

SHANNON: Much of the ambiguity in these stories centres on an uncertainty around time and reality. We see characters drift between being awake and dreaming, the lines blurring as time goes on. In "Dosette Box," Scarlett has no circadian rhythm, sleeping when the mood hits, breaking the reader's sense of what is happening when. Dreams start to make more sense than reality, providing a window into what is, for the characters, both a worst fear and a secret desire. In "Spiderling," dreams portray the protagonist's terror of losing control, and wish to be free from the need to feel in control.

AMBER: Ultimately, any story can feature slow burn horror; the genre only defines a narrative's pacing and atmosphere. For this anthology, we also chose a uniting theme: household horror. Just like keeping eggs in a room they don't belong in, our aim was to take normal elements of domesticity and place them in an environment that is just unexpected enough to feel wrong.

Household horror forces us to look within, at the day-to-day things we take for granted.

> *"Imagine that we are sitting in an ordinary room. Suddenly we are told that there is a corpse behind the door. In an instant the room we are sitting in is completely altered; everything in it has taken on another look; the light, the atmosphere have changed, though they are physically the same. This is because we have changed, and the objects are as we conceive them."*
>
> CARL DREYER

SHANNON: Household horror disrupts routine, makes family strangers, turns the home unfamiliar and safe spaces untrustworthy. In short, it makes the mundane unsettling. Each writer in the anthology explored these ideas. The protagonist in "Spiderling" expresses his control issues through his routine, so the story forces him out of it. "Dosette Box" is about a young woman on the cusp of adult life, forced to regress from an expected milestone. Tokki in "1999: Year of the Rabbit" is an unknowable force and the grandmother, daughter, grandaughter trio in "Tapes" couldn't be more out of touch. The house in "Within Walls" is more threatening than comforting and despite spending the entire story in the comfort of her decked-out kitchen, the protagonist in "Not a River" is not safe.

AMBER: Because the stories in this anthology are, at their

core, about households, they have a strong sense of space. Characters are often stuck in their spaces, whether in a room, a nursery, or on a sofa. They begin to blend with them. From "Fungal": "They've been lying on this couch for so long it's as though they've become fused with it." As part of the writing process, this saw the writers in this anthology placing much more emphasis on setting. Shannon based her stories on locations she knew; Georgie made a map of the apartment in "Spaces."

SHANNON: Many of these stories are personal, dredging up fears connected to our everyday lives. I transformed my experience getting my Wisdom teeth removed into "Fungal." My struggle with eczema became the itch that haunts the protagonist of "Slow Burn."

AMBER: "Dosette Box" is my response to my hospitalization after university, after experiencing the horror of feeling that I had entered adulthood only to have my body turn on me as I ended up back in nappies and entirely reliant on others. Like Scarlett, I was bed-bound, housebound, and had a seriously warped concept of time. My world for months was shrunk down to a three-bedroom terraced house in Norwich.

SHANNON: Across the anthology, you'll see a running theme of transitional times—divorce, unemployment, childbirth. But specifically, a lot of the milestones represented in the stories are those of early adulthood: moving in with a serious partner for the first time, graduating university, getting your first job. It should come as no surprise to someone reading the stories in this collection that they were written by a group of twenty-somethings not long out of university. "Slow Burn" is about a recently unemployed young woman who is ostensibly job hunting, but primarily ambling around aimlessly, terrified of looking at her CV and uncertain what comes next. Can you tell I wrote it when I was between jobs? Even in the stories that seem more detached from personal experience, there's a prevailing anxiety over loss of control that feels reminiscent of early adult life. The themes of parenthood that run through "One Candle," "1999: Year of the Rabbit," and "Kill Your Youngest" speak to a discomfort towards the future. The characters in "Within Walls" and "Spaces" find themselves needing to build homes from scratch. The cosmic dread in "Not a River" is more like set dressing; the real fear rooted in an anxiety about adult responsibilities and being unable to fulfill them.

Amber: There's also a running theme of isolation throughout the collection. Ingrid and the baby have been alone for many years; Anna Williams' four-person house is abandoned more often than not. Isolation is a common companion to horror because it provides a good setup. But further, I think it speaks to the fact that many of these stories were written and edited between 2020 and 2022, when a global pandemic completely reshaped the way people can interact with the world. It was a prevailing mood of the time, and it's a prevailing mood of early adulthood, this terror and loneliness at the idea of entering adult life and realizing you are the master of your destiny. Decisions are entirely yours to be made. There is no one but you who can bear witness to the horrors you experience.

SHANNON: Going back to my anecdote about keeping eggs in the bedroom, I think a large part of what drew me to the imagery was the fact that it wasn't clear why it bothered me. Horror provides a place for us to explore our fears, our discomforts. It is where we can grapple with the unknown and unknowable. There are rules to adult life that are unspoken, all-consuming, and not often logical. Why did it feel like my roommate taking eggs from his bedroom was breaking a rule? What are the rules that I have accepted, unthinking, as the borders of correct living? In this project, the five of us seek to answer that question.

> *"For the most wild yet most homely narrative which I am about to pen, I neither expect nor solicit belief. Mad indeed would I be to expect it, in a case where my very senses reject their own evidence. Yet, mad am I not—and very surely do I not dream. But to-morrow I die, and to-day I would unburden my soul. My immediate purpose is to place before the world, plainly, succinctly, and without comment, a series of mere household events."*
>
> EDGAR ALLAN POE, "THE BLACK CAT"

Introduction:
On Atmosphere

Dr Jacob Huntley

THE WRITER ROBERT HUGH BENSON ONCE said the atmosphere supernatural fiction should evoke was "like looking at the backs of a crowd; they are attending to something else, not us at all. Just occasionally we catch the eye of some who turn round—but that is all." The suggestion that something is somehow wrong, or off, yet the source of that sensation cannot be easily seen or distinguished, is the definition of the uncanny. The golden age of the ghost story—roughly from the latter few decades of the nineteenth century to the initial twenty years or so of the twentieth—saw that emphasis on mood and atmosphere highlighted through unsettled or unsettling environments or disturbed senses. Houses or individual rooms imbued with chilliness or dolorous feelings, everyday objects with just a bit too much animation, things that should be still yet possessing a disquieting appearance of sentience, or the persisting nag of déjà vu. There was nearly always in such stories, or at least the best of them, what M. R. James referred to as a loophole, an escape route into the safety of the enlightened every day, even if its unlikelihood couldn't fully expunge the preceding spookiness. Faced with shadows across the window or the creaking stairs within the empty building, queasy uncertainty cannot be easily dismissed, and once it's under the skin, one can't shake it off.

How much worse when what one anxiously anticipates is confirmed. There is no one present, even though the doorbell is being pressed and sounding with clamorous urgency. The dwindling sunlight reveals one shadow too few. Yes, the dead thing is now moving again. And its groping ambulation is coming ever close to you. Horror, then, is bound up with the shock of an encounter with the repugnant or the abject. Horripilation, the goose-pimpling of skin, confirms the corporeality at play: the body reacts in disgust to disgust. The popular perception of the horror genre today is perhaps governed by the pervasiveness of the tradition of film and its attendant media. In a culture essentially trained in scopophilia, the horrific spectacle becomes privileged. It is the sight of Lon Chaney's Phantom, his mask plucked away by Mary Philbin's tremulous Christine, that caused fainting fits among the 1920s audience. The lurid Technicolor blood spurting from Christopher Lee's eye in *The Curse of Frankenstein* equally piqued and repulsed audiences in 1957 and rejuvenated Hammer Films; the shocking scene of the gunshot resulting in the garish, glaring red from the wound hooks together in a commercial film the threat to sight lingering in what is an essentially visual medium. (The lurking ommetaphobia was already there in 1929's *Un Chien Andalou*, where a cloud covering the moon transitions to its bodily analogue of a razor slicing an eyeball, and even in the medium's infancy George Meliere's 1902 film *Le Voyage Dans La Lune* features a rocket fired towards the moon's face, which lands in the right eye.)

Horror as a genre is not just localised to the ocular, however. Disgust, shock, fright, or the shivers may be elicited from readers as much as viewers, and the enduring tradition of horror fiction results from the imaginative representation of descriptive detail, often in combination or employing association. The beached SS Demeter with its cargo of mould-filled wooden boxes, piloted by a corpse bound to the wheel, from which an immense dog leaps to land, might make no narrative sense (why would Dracula seemingly try to thwart his own plan of journeying to Britain?) yet it provides a gruesome tableau of death, decay, metamorphosis, and threat. It's a set piece that can be recognised and appreciated by afficionados of the genre, and part of that enjoyment comes from the inferences developed by the reader from the implications supplied by the writer. It's what was in a wooden box that escapes the ship, having caused the surviving terrified sailor to tether himself to the wheel, the horrific proximity to the vampire being known to the reader if not The Dailygraph correspondent, coastguard, and the others exploring the vessel.

Maybe this particular feature of the horror genre

is part of its ongoing appeal: for all the gore, splatter, or monstrosity that provokes the immediacy of reaction, the genre's surface effects celebrated by fans and condemned by its detractors, there might be more horror that's insidious, latent; there might be something concealed or camouflaged in the subtextual. Mary Shelley's animated assemblage of human and animal parts snags at multiple cultural fears, personifying anxieties that might not easily be articulated. It may appear grisly enough when Charlotte Perkins Gilman's narrator stares at wallpaper where "the pattern lolls like a broken neck and two bulbous eyes," yet the greater horror is the subtle perception of the "faint figure" of a woman imprisoned behind, the belated recognition of her social and matrimonial entrapment.

Happily, for readers, surface and the subtext can be extensively employed by writers of horror fiction. In the old currency of Freudian methodology, both latent and manifest content are at the writer's disposal, delimited only by their imaginative capabilities. And of course, in horror, states of being may not be stable. The nightmare can extrude into the waking world, the vanquished monster may disappear in order to recur. A writer alert to the possibilities of the scenario they have created, and deft in their descriptive abilities, can immerse their reader in an experience both persuasive and frightening.

As a case in point, this present anthology. Very much a fresh irruption of creative horror fiction rather than a disinterment, this promises myriad interpretations of what can scare, unsettle, and jolt our senses. *Slow*

Burn has been put together by former students at UEA, who already have a fine track record, having produced *Octarine* magazine whilst studying. What exactly is lurking within the duck pond in Helen's new garden in "Not a River"? The thing bumping at the cat-flap can only be disquieting. In "Kill Your Youngest," the image of boiled horse bones turning over in the pot like driftwood braids together more than one source of disgust. In the grand tradition of the genre, settle down to be unsettled.

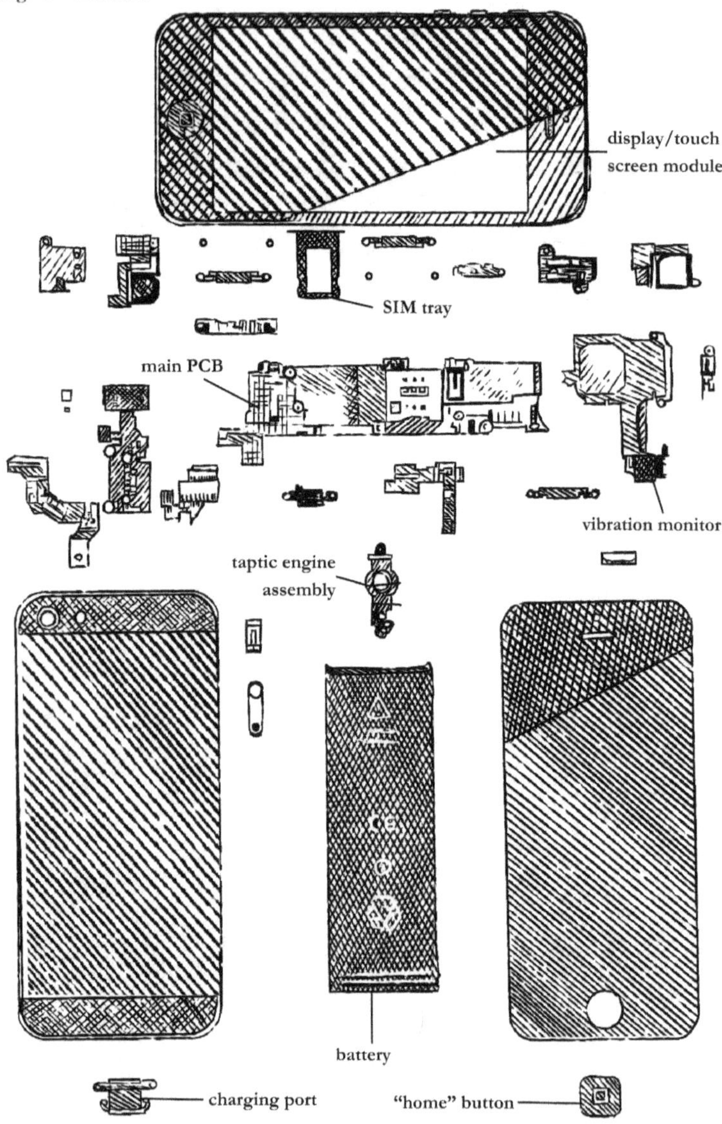

Fig. 1 — iPhone 5
display/touch
screen module
SIM tray
main PCB
vibration monitor
taptic engine
assembly
battery
charging port
"home" button

Fungal

Shannon Lewis

THEY HAVE BEEN LYING PROSTRATE BEFORE the television for three days now. Maybe four. They've lost track a little. Gingerly, they run a finger over their swollen jawline. It is definitely much better than the first, or especially the second, day. The dentist had warned them that day two was always the worst and yet they'd still been surprised to find a distended face staring back in the mirror. Their cheeks looked like overripe pears, mottled and bruised.

Sleep comes to them in waves. Their schedule has broken free of the constraints of daylight. The cold glow of the television sustains them through the night. The only thing that marks the passage of time is the painkillers they swallow every six or eight hours. A few doses ago, they can't remember which, they accidentally doubled up. The lines of the room went wavy and they had a dream they were sitting on the couch watching TV. It was barely a dream and they wouldn't have noticed they were asleep except they couldn't move because there were thin tendrils wrapped around their wrists, holding them in place. When they eventually opened their eyes, the tendrils were gone but the television was still there. National Geographic. Something about the Malheur National Forest in Oregon. It's home, the television informs them in a soothing voice, to the world's biggest living organism. Armillaria ostoyae. It covers almost four square miles of forest floor, communicating via a subterranean web of roots called mycelium. Now that's a humongous fungus, jokes the narrator, deadpan. The forest name comes up on the screen again. Something stirs in the back of their mind. Long-forgotten French lessons from when they were a teen. Malheur. Misfortune. A strange name for a park.

They try to move and it takes their muscles a moment to respond. They've been lying on this couch for so long it's as though they've become fused with it. Whenever they do move, four lumps at the top and bottom of their jaw throb hot. When the X-rays came through, their dentist almost laughed. Every tooth was coming in in a different and equally wrong direction. They were still a ways away from wreaking havoc, she explained, pointing at the perfect outline embedded in the translucent image of their gums, but it wasn't worth waiting until they did. It was on the dentist's recommendation that they got all four removed at once. I did my daughter's two at a time, she said, and boy did she regret having to go through this twice.

In the bathroom, they pour a tiny cup of water and drink half of it alongside two small white pills. The other half they swill and spit out. It is a soft pink, swirled with red blood and frothy saliva. They swallow. They can feel the stitches threaded through their gums. They weren't supposed to talk at all for the first few days, so as not to rip them out. That was no problem. There's no one to talk to. It is just them, the television, and the couch. It's been four, or maybe only three days and they haven't made a noise.

Back in the living room, they turn up the heat. Before the surgery, they went through the entire house turning off every radiator except the ones in the living room. Their nest is a tiny hot pocket in a frozen landscape. Mould central, Aunt Hazel would have called it. They've always hated the house, yet Hazel had left it to them anyway when she died. Years ago, when Hazel was still well, it was always cold. She kept the windows open to prevent the spread of an insidious black mould in corners of rooms and crevices between tile. As the years went by, Hazel left the house less and less often. Hours scouring websites about agoraphobia bore no results. Hazel had no problem with the outside; she just preferred to stay in. That was what she said anyway. During that time, the house was always warm. Unbearably warm. Hazel would refuse to open any windows at all. She said she didn't want it escaping. Every shower, every kettle of tea filled the house with a steam that could go nowhere. It seeped into the walls.

They blink several times. With the curtains closed, it is hard to know how much time has passed. They closed them the first day, for sure, when they arrived home with a mouth full of blood and a head full of cotton. At that time, the light had seemed insulting. Excessive. Now, they probably wouldn't mind a little sunlight, but that would involve getting up, which seems wholly unnecessary. They glance at their phone to check the time. The battery is low, a thin red sliver, but the charger is all the way upstairs. They haven't even made the journey there for bedtime, choosing instead to pass out on the couch whenever the whim hits. They put their phone back down on a table then realize they never checked the time.

Aunt Hazel's house had needed a runthrough by a professional cleaning service by the time it passed onto them. Even after that, for months they kept the windows wide open. The rooms smelled of mildew, the halls of earth. Hazel had died of ringworm, a disease that until then they had always associated with cats. They didn't even realize humans could get it. Well, technically she hadn't died of ringworm. It had been an infection caused by the ringworm. But it didn't matter the exact cause. By that point, Hazel had been gone for at least a year. By then, she was always talking about herself and her house as if she wasn't alone. When she tried to invite them over on the phone, it was always, "we would love to have you." They tried telling themselves it was the royal "we," some affectation picked up after watching too many Christmas speeches, but it never convinced them. It had been a closed casket service.

Their tongue runs over the gaps at the back of their mouth. It's been doing that a lot since the swelling went down. They can't help it. They keep trying to place how it must look, but it feels impossible to imagine. It is a divot in bone stretched over by pliable wet gum. A tiny abyss within them. They think back to when they were young and losing baby teeth. They used to love it. The attention a loose tooth got, the coins hidden beneath pillows. They used to save loose teeth for when they got bored in class until one day one of their teeth was dangling by a single pink thread and they were trying to make it last because it was one of the final baby teeth they had left but the time had come. The teacher was writing scores of long division on the whiteboard. They began to twist, expecting it to come loose immediately like a popped soda cap. But it didn't. They twisted again. It held fast. They twisted and twisted but the tooth refused to pull loose of its root. They tried the other way round. It didn't matter. A panic was setting in. They imagined themselves living the rest of their life with a full set of shiny white adult teeth and this one dangling monstrosity. They twisted harder, tugging. They must have burst something because droplets of blood began falling on the graph paper before them, blurring the pencil numbers. By this point, their teacher noticed. A scold died on his lips when he saw how panicked they were. Then it was straight to the paramedic who tried pulling and twisting before giving up and snipping the loose strand with a sterilized pair of surgical scissors. When it was finished, it lay in the paramedic's gloved hand, tiny, white, a pink coil around it like an umbilical cord. They had refused to take it home, didn't even tell their mother it had come out. They never left anything for the tooth fairy after that. The thought of some fae being pocketing their teeth suddenly made them feel very sick.

Their tongue runs over a lump and their blood turns to slush. They have been exploring their traumatised gum for days now. A lump is new. They run their tongue over it again. It's thin like a subcutaneous thread. Before they can think about it too much, the television plays tinkling music. It announces a third part to the show they were watching about creatures great and small. They blink. A day must have gone by. The series only airs once a day. A dull ache runs through their mouth. Pain medicine. They scramble for their phone, where they set an alarm to go off at every dosage. It's dead, a cool block.

They get up and go to the bathroom. Their joints ache, a thready feeling passing through them. Even as they take steps, they can still feel their form laying on the sofa. Their existence seems to span past their one body. When they get to the bathroom, they notice how bad the mould in the upper corner has got. It's freezing compared to the living room; they have no idea how it can survive. When they look in the mirror, they smile, checking the damage.

On their gum, just above the right-hand front tooth, is a white speck. They lean in closer to inspect, raising a finger to it. A damp feeling passes through them as they realize the white is tooth poking out through gum. As soon as they touch it, the hole grows. Their gum begins to burn away, dissolving from that initial speck outward until there is no pink. They cannot stop it. The top of their mouth is all tooth, long and white and gone in an instant. They blink and their mouth is back to normal. They blink again and, to their horror, they have no teeth. They blink. The teeth come back. They blink. The teeth are all loose, clinging to their spots by pink tendrils.

They run back to the living room. Their tongue inspects the teeth, which all seem in order except the divots at the back of the mouth. There is a swelling under them, a small lump that they can move a little if they exert enough pressure. The television is telling them about mushroom spores. Every black dot is actually a collection of thousands of spores. An individual spore is invisible to the human eye.

They learned about fungus for the first time in year four, a lesson on the classification of living things. Until that point, they'd always thought of mushrooms as a vegetable no different from a carrot or a blade of grass. When their teacher said fungus was its own classification, they'd refused to believe it. They'd asked their mum, but she said she didn't know the difference and to trust the teacher. They'd asked Aunt Hazel and she'd responded, "What did you expect?"

From that moment, every new thing they learned about fungus seemed more horrible than the last. Once, after their first and final brush with cocaine in college, they had tried to explain the horrifying classification to their then-girlfriend. She hadn't understood what the problem was, so they'd ended up spending hours Googling information about fungus to try to freak her out. Nothing had worked until they found a fact about how mushrooms don't feed off sunlight like plants. Like animals, the page proclaimed, they need to get their food from other organisms.

They readjust. Somehow, they know they are laying in the exact same position they have been for five days now. Or has it been six? They check their phone, but remember it's dead right as they press the home button. They feel like an inverted puppet. Rather than dangling from overhead strings, they are tied down, a series of threads keeping them in place against the Earth's surface. If they close their eyes, they can trace the exact steps they took to get to the bathroom. They can see each footprint outlined on the floor. Their tongue runs over the lumps at the back of their mouth. One seems to have burst free of the gum. It is a tougher texture, yet somehow more pliable. Foamy, almost. They should call the dentist and let her know, but their phone is dead and the charger is upstairs. They can feel upstairs, sense the exact place where the charger lay through phantom fingers. But it's so far and the couch has molded perfectly to the shape of their body.

Hazel might have died in this very spot. The thought crosses their mind before they can stop it. They've been dancing around it for years. Hazel died in the house. They knew it and didn't know it. Now there is no unknowing it. With the curtains closed, in this tight warm room, it feels as though Hazel is less dead than she has been in half a decade. They can feel every step Hazel took through the house, they can feel how she lay in that very spot, her arms and legs at the exact same angles and crooks as theirs. Every breath they take they know is in time with one of Hazel's. They once read about how oxygen is not generated, only recycled. Their air and her air are one and the same.

The television grows louder. They have no idea where the remote is nor what is causing it. It says, "From the largest colony to the smallest spore, there is a fungus among us." They nestle down, feeling every step that goes through the house, that went through the house. It has been six days, or maybe seven. They don't remember when they last ate. Their tongue runs over the lumps in their mouth. Each is filled with this tuber-like root wiring their mouth shut. It doesn't matter. There is no one to speak to, not with words. The house smells of dirt. Somehow they know that the roots in their mouth travel through their body, down past the couch and scuffed wooden floor, all the way to deep within the earth. Somewhere, a mile away, a squirrel runs across a grassy knoll. They know. They can feel it. Everything in the earth is them and not them.

The air is thick, soupy. Invisible spores flow in and out of pumping lungs, coursing through veins, curling around the aorta of a heart. Our mycelium span distances ordinary people can't imagine. The spot where their teeth were yanked without ceremony might throb, but we feel no pain. What is pain?

We do not know how much time has passed. We are not hungry, but we are always feeding. We rise from the sofa, our form moving and stagnant. We turn off the television, the thrumming lights. In the dark, in the warm, we are safe. Our phone is dead, our aunt is dead, our teeth are gone. Our gums burn away like acid. Every mycelium is like a nerve ending and every nerve ending speaks to another. Beneath the ground, there is a web that spans the planet, ever growing, ever speaking, ever us. Comforted, never alone again, we lay back down in the spot, the exact spot with the crook of a leg and adjustment of a cushion, where we have spent the past seven days, maybe eight.

Fig. 2 — knife and celery

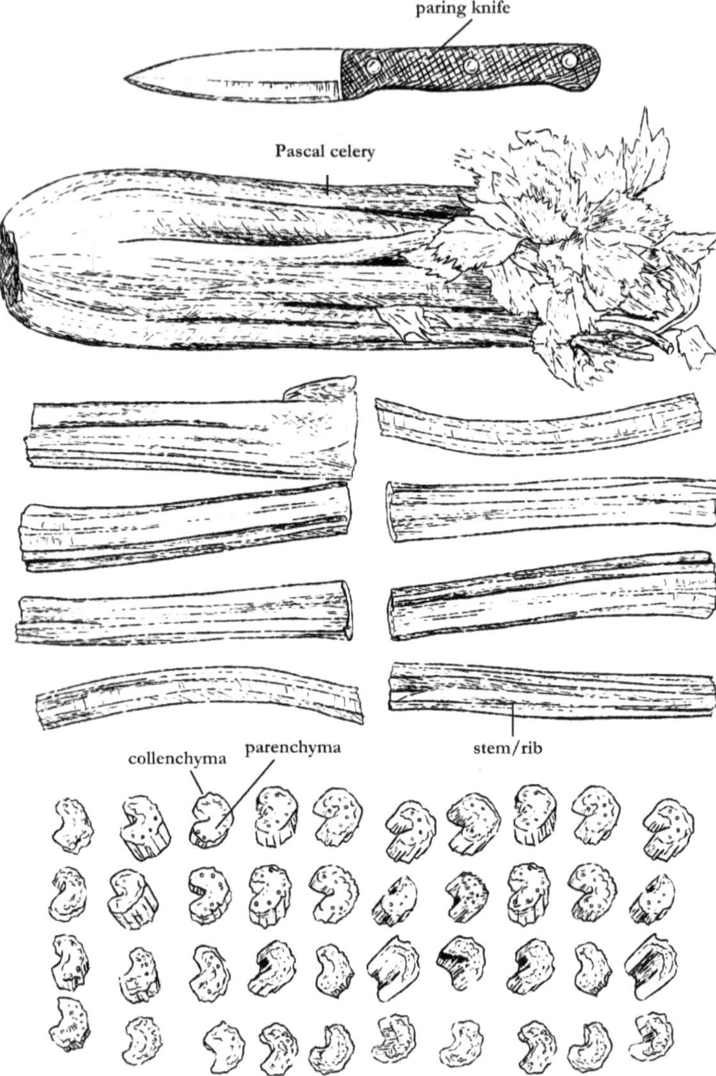
paring knife
Pascal celery
collenchyma
parenchyma
stem/rib

1999: Year of the Rabbit

Kathryn Leigh

HANGING ON THE WALL OUTSIDE MY PSY-chologist's office was a painting. A grey square with a black circle in the middle. I stared at it, playing with the button on my shirtsleeve. It was really a horrible painting. It reminded me of frogspawn, some-how.

"It's my first time seeing a psychologist." I said when I entered the room. His name was Dr Kim. I wondered how many people felt like they needed to say that during their first appointment.

"What brings you here today?" Dr Kim asked, resting his hands on the desk. I glanced out the window. The sun was shining; the sky a gentle blue mottled with clouds.

"I'm having some difficulties in my life." I said, which was an understatement. I couldn't remember what I had written in my preliminary forms.

Dr Kim had an ageless face but I thought he was

probably older than me. "What sort of difficulties?"

"I'm trying to raise my younger brother, but I think there's something wrong with him. Or me. That's why I'm here. I need someone to help me understand."

Dr Kim had very knowing eyes. "I will certainly try." He said.

I was living in a small house with my little brother Tokki. We lived there alone because both of our parents had died in a tragic road accident ten years prior. For the first five years after they died, we tried to keep living in the family home we'd inherited. Eventually it all became too much, so we moved to the small house.

"It all became too much, you said?"

"All the books and articles said it would be a good idea to have a clear out. But the more we cleared out, the more upset we were and the more hopeless of a challenge it seemed. It was just bags and boxes and piles of them."

"Your parents?"

"Yes. Everywhere. I remember Tokki grabbing handfuls of this old chicken wire and slicing his hand open with it. We had to go to the hospital, and it sounds terrible but it was almost a relief. We decided in the waiting room that it was just more trouble than it was worth. We should just move. We could move closer to the new school."

Whenever I thought about that day I remembered the yellow iodine they dabbed on Tokki's injury and how when the taxi dropped us home there had been a trail of blood dots like wax seals leading right up to the door of our parents' house. I had tried to take Tokki's hand without thinking and he'd flinched.

"Tokki was moving schools?" Dr Kim asked.

"Yes. He was going to high school. It came at the right time. He'd gotten into some...issues at the previous school."

"Why was that exactly?"

"Don't misunderstand, Tokki was always good in school. He wasn't too smart but he was good at running. But he just has these eyes. Girls always liked him, and Tokki....well. I think he liked girls too much. Some of my friends' siblings went to the same school, and my friends would tell me, 'Oh your little brother, he only wants one thing.' And I tried to speak to him about it but he was fourteen, you know? It was so embarrassing."

"I see."

"He's no different at the new school. But I think because he's older people don't care so much. Or they don't say anything, at least."

I felt too ashamed to describe in detail the one time I tried to lecture Tokki about this, how my ill-conceived speech began with "when I was your age, I wouldn't have dared," how I remembered too late that when I was his age, I wasn't an orphan sifting through the detritus of my dead parents. And how at the end, without looking at me, he said:

"I see. You're jealous because you're a virgin."

Tokki and I argued the night after I got back from the first therapy session. I bought us fried chicken but he refused to eat.

"You know I don't eat meat."

"I thought that was just temporary. Like a detox."

"It wasn't a 'detox.' Meat is disgusting. Do you do this on purpose?"

I didn't know what to say because yes, I did do it on purpose, because I was concerned that Tokki's diet of rice balls and green smoothies did not contain enough protein. He scoffed and rolled his eyes at my silence and stomped down into the basement, where his bedroom was. Back when we were looking for places to live, Tokki was excited at the idea of having a basement room. At first I didn't understand the appeal of living underground, but when I thought about it, a boy having scandalous relationships with the girls in his school might want a windowless room. Or a room as far away from mine as possible. He would bring a different girl over every couple of weeks, shamelessly, and I always thought they seemed sweet. Then they would get tired of him. He never shed a tear over it.

"Do you feel concerned about losing control over your brother as he grows up?" Dr Kim took a sip of coffee. I was dying for a cigarette.

"I don't know. I do get worried, because he seems very unwise."

"You mean with regards to sex?"

"It's like there's nothing at all behind his eyes. You know, the other day when I got home from work there was a man leaving the house. I'm sure it was someone Tokki met on the internet."

"I see. Let's leave Tokki aside for now. Has anything been happening in *your* life?"

I felt irritated at Dr Kim for a moment. Everything that happened in my life was either boring or involved my brother.

"I've been having a recurring nightmare."

"Oh yes?"

"I'm inside my parents house during a storm, and my mother's gone into labour and gone with my father to the hospital. It makes sense, because it really did happen like that. Tokki was born the night of a terrible storm, and I waited at home. I think my uncle was meant to come and watch me but a tree got blown into his driveway. Anyway, in the dream, instead of my parents bringing a baby home at the end, the police arrive and tell me that there's been an accident."

"Your parents died in a car accident, correct?" Dr Kim turned a page of his file on me briefly, and I saw my own handwriting. I wished I could remember what I had already told him.

"Yes, ten years ago. I was eighteen."

"It says here that you feel guilty about what happened."

I sighed. "I don't feel guilty like it was my fault. I feel bad for the situation. For the fact that Tokki has to grow up with no parents and I didn't."

"You don't consider yourself his parent?"

The question surprised me. "No. I didn't make him. He was just given to me."

"You chose to raise him for all these years, when you would have been within your rights to refuse."

"When I was nine years old, my parents bought me a rabbit. I was never any good at looking after it. After that I decided I would never raise anything more complicated than a succulent."

"And yet here you are."

I shrugged.

One night between that appointment and my next, I heard a strange noise coming from downstairs. It was a hot, still night. I got out of bed and walked down the stairs. The streetlamp outside shone a weak orange light into the hallway, the trees in the garden casting shadows across the floor. I followed the sound, a rhythmic scraping coming from Tokki's room. It was similar to a chair being dragged back and forth on a hard floor. I hesitated, then remembered that I was the responsible one in this house. I knocked on the door. The scraping stopped. I waited for Tokki to come to the door, but he didn't appear. I waited a little more and then saw on the hallway clock that it was past two and decided to just call it a success and go back to bed. Before I managed to get back to sleep, the sound began again, quieter, but just discernible over the usual creakings of the house. I stormed down the stairs.

"Tokki! Open this door."

The scraping stopped immediately. I heard shuffling and the door opened to reveal my younger brother. His black hair was in disarray, and his large eyes were bloodshot and puffy with sleep. He was eating sunflower seeds from his left hand.

"Is there someone down there? Why are you awake?"

He looked up at me with narrowed eyes. "No one's here. I had a nightmare."

"You did?" I felt sorry for accusing him. Me too, I wanted to say.

"Yeah. I was in a cage, looking up at mum. You were there, too. I dunno." He threw the rest of the sunflower seeds into his mouth and licked the salt off the palm of his hand, where the scar from the chicken wire was still visible.

———◇———

Dr Kim seemed genuinely intrigued. "And you've had this same nightmare?"

"Yeah. I'm trapped in a cage, and I see my mother looking down at me. Then I see Tokki looking at me from far away. I'm terrified but he just stares right at me.”

"But he didn't mention seeing himself. He says he saw you."

I had never been good at recalling my dreams. Now, when I thought back to the boy I saw, it was difficult to tell whether it was a younger Tokki or a younger me. People always said we looked similar. Sometimes, in childhood photographs, we couldn't tell ourselves apart.

"I mean, Tokki and I looked alike when we were younger. It doesn't matter anyway, they're just dreams."

"Yes, quite. It's possible you were both influenced by the same stimulus. A movie or book, perhaps."

"Tokki and I haven't been to see a movie in a while."

"Perhaps you should."

We sat awkwardly at opposite ends of the sofa. An animated movie was playing—*Watership Down*. It wasn't either of our first choices, but we had very specific requirements. I vetoed sex, gore, and anything really cryptic. Tokki vetoed romance, comedy, and anything longer than two hours. The one thing we agreed on was that it had to be something we hadn't seen before. The film seemed cute at first, but I was beginning to feel like it fell into my forbidden genres. We watched in silence. Tokki seemed very tired.

"Is everything going well at school?" I asked. I saw him nod out of the corner of my eye, and then yawn so widely I heard his jaw crack.

Halfway through the movie, I decided to come clean.

"My therapist actually suggested this. I'm sorry if it's awkward." I muttered.

Tokki stared straight ahead, black eyes reflecting the screen. "It's not what I expected."

The lights flickered and went out. The movie went silent.

"Oh. Another power cut?" Tokki murmured, still watching the dead TV.

"Maybe just the fuse. I'll go." I said, fumbling my way in the dark.

The fuse box was downstairs in Tokki's bedroom. I half-expected him to stop me going there, but he didn't move from the sofa. Everything looked very grey and sudden in the light of my phone torch. The stairs down to the basement were very steep, and smelled like him. The fuse box in the corner had a little red light blinking on it. Something about the air in the basement made me sneeze; through my blurred vision, the fuse box had two little red blinking eyes. I shook my head, touched the fuse box, opened it, flicked the correct fuse. The lights upstairs came back on, illuminating the top of the basement stairs. Through the floor I heard the sounds of the film coming back to life.

It was still dark in Tokki's bedroom. I stood there for a moment. His bed was just a mattress on the floor. It was neatly made, the duvet decorated with a tiny checked pattern that looked a little like a chain link fence. On the walls were dozens of posters. Idol groups I was too old to know, a dated *Playboy* pin-up. There was a half-empty mug and a plate with celery leaves on the desk, alongside an open biology textbook and the white, clean skull of a small animal. I recoiled, then put my hand out to touch it. It was dry and slightly cool beneath my finger, and definitely real. I suddenly felt sick. I took the crockery up the stairs, intending to ask Tokki where he'd gotten a skull from but when I entered the living room he was asleep. The light from the television flickered green and blue across his slack face. I put the plate in the kitchen, and when I turned around, a rabbit on the television was ripping another rabbit's throat out; the red shone on Tokki's hair. I went and sat down next to him, not watching the screen. When the film ended I sat and stared out the window.

"You didn't speak to him about the animal skull?"

"I couldn't. It felt like we were finally getting along."

"Why would bringing it up have made you fall out?"

"Two years ago, something happened—"

The blinds rattled urgently. Dr Kim raised his eyebrow. "Excuse me." He stood up, crossed the room and closed the window. Grey clouds were racing across the sky, with a bank of black ones on the horizon.

"Is it meant to storm today?" I asked, regretting bringing up the incident.

Dr Kim sat down, placing his pencil in the crease between the two pages of his notebook. "Please continue."

"I already took him to therapy. And they assured me there was nothing wrong with him."

"Sir, I am not here to judge what you did or did not do. I am just here to listen, and help."

I felt a bead of sweat run down my back.

"Excuse me for a moment." I said, and left the room. There was a bathroom at the end of the corridor. I went and locked myself inside. It smelled of bleach. I splashed cold water on my face, and stared at myself in the mirror. I looked exhausted, and not in the least like my younger brother. I had five o'clock shadow and felt decades older than twenty-eight. I steeled myself and headed back to the therapy room. As I approached the office door I caught a glimpse of the ugly painting I noticed on the day of my first appointment, an eternity ago. The black circle in the middle of the grey square was bigger than I remembered. The corridor lights flickered and the circle seemed to dilate like a pupil. I went into the office and sat down. Dr Kim was sitting very still, like he hadn't moved at all since I left.

"Okay. I was sitting at home. It was two days after Tokki's sixteenth birthday." I sat on the edge of the chair, not looking at Dr Kim. "It was the evening. Tokki was in his room, playing computer games. Someone started knocking at the door, so I went and answered it and it was a middle aged couple I didn't recognise. So I said, how can I help you? And they said that I was lucky they hadn't called the police, and was Tokki here? I said yes, and what were they talking about? They said that Tokki was clearly disturbed, and that if they ever caught him near their daughter again then they would call the police. Obviously I realised then that this must be one of Tokki's girlfriend's parents. So I asked what exactly he had done, and they said—" My voice shook. I tried to visualise a calm void, but it looked just like the horrible painting outside.

Dr Kim's hands rested near the pencil, but they didn't pick it up.

"They said that he had killed her pet rabbit."

An eyebrow raise. "And had he?"

"She had an indoor rabbit. Tokki was in her bedroom, and she went to the kitchen to get some snacks. When she came back, the rabbit was dead and Tokki was gone."

"That is very strange. It isn't possible that it died of natural causes?"

"They showed me a picture. There was a lot of blood."

I had tried many times in the years since to forget the blurry image of the grey rabbit with its filmy eyes, fur covered in blood, blood on the carpet beneath it.

"Do you think he did it?"

"I called him up out of the basement, obviously. His girlfriend's parents wouldn't even cross the threshold. He stared at them and then at me. When they accused him, he just said, 'Why would I do that?' He never outright denied it, but there was obviously no evidence that he had. And…Tokki has always been strange, but never violent. I never believed he could do something like that."

"Until you found the animal skull in his bedroom."

"I don't know how that got there. I don't know why. And I don't want to ask. I took him to a therapist and they said there's nothing wrong with him."

"He has been through some traumatic things. You both have. Sometimes these things manifest. Not that I am accusing him." Dr Kim leaned back in his chair. "Traumatic incidents can cause anger."

"There was a time, about a year after the funeral, when Tokki would say, 'our parents didn't die, they were killed.' I used to get angry at him for saying that. I told him, the police said it seemed like they swerved to avoid something in the road. But the rain was so bad they skidded into the wall. It was a tragic accident, but it was nobody's fault. The weather's fault, maybe. I read online that sometimes children like to project, when they have been through something they don't understand…"

I realised as I was saying this that my cheeks were wet. Dr Kim handed me a box of tissues. My hand shook as I gripped the box, its corner digging into my palm.

"I killed the rabbit," I said.

Dr Kim sat up straight once again.

"You killed the rabbit?"

"Not Jaein's rabbit. I have no idea how that happened. I killed my rabbit when I was a kid. It was the night Tokki was born. My parents drove off to have him, and I don't remember whether they told me to bring the rabbit inside or not. Obviously they had other things to think about. But the storm was so bad I didn't want to go outside. I remember opening the door and looking out at the cage, and seeing the rabbit in there. When the lightning flashed I couldn't see anything at all. The rain was so heavy it was deafening, and the wind kept trying to blow the door wide open. So I shut it and locked it, and ate cereal and watched cartoons. My uncle never showed up, but I didn't care. I fell asleep on the sofa, and when I woke up the storm had blown over, but I looked outside and saw the rabbit lying there dead."

"What did you do?"

"The chicken wire cage had half lifted up from the wind. I just pulled the rabbit out and put it in the gap between the fence and the garden shed. I hoped my parents would just think it had escaped. When they came back with the baby that was the first thing I said to them, 'The rabbit escaped!' It was obvious, really. But they weren't upset with me. They just said, 'you have a brother to look after now,' and showed him to me."

"And do you feel guilty about that?"

"It's the only thing in my life that I regret." I said, taking a tissue from the box. "If I could go back and change one thing, I would bring the rabbit inside."

Dr Kim finally picked up his pencil and began to write something. Then the power went out. We were both plunged into darkness.

"For fuck's sake." Dr Kim said. We sat there for a few minutes, until it became clear the power was not going to come back on.

Dr Kim stood up. "It's probably best if we both head out before we get stranded. It's going to be chaos on the trains. Unless you'd like to continue your appointment in the dark." He fumbled on the desk for something.

I turned on my phone torch. "No, that's alright. We only had ten minutes left."

"Ah, thank you. Perhaps I should invest in a new phone for such situations."

I glanced out the window. The sky was the colour of a bruised plum, occasionally punctuated by the silhouette of a bird or a spinning leaf. Dr Kim had his coat on, and was standing by the door.

"Please lead the way," he said. I scuttled past him, phone held ahead of me.

We parted ways at the door to the building, which Dr Kim shared with numerous therapists and other professionals in need of small office space.

"I'll see you at your next appointment, then."

"Yes."

"I think we made progress today." Dr Kim nodded, the wind snatching the words and making them sound insincere.

I wanted to reply, but there was an enormous roll of thunder and rain began falling in earnest. We both turned and went our separate ways. I felt enormous guilt at having revealed Tokki's secret. When I emerged from the subway, rain was lashing down. I had no hood so my hair was soaked through within moments. The gutters were like tiny fast-flowing rivers. The rain hurtled

sideways, leaves and branches scattered across the pavement like limbs. I thought of Tokki, alone in the house.
I remembered the nightmare, trapped in a cage while the
sky turned purple above.

Our house looked very small and crooked when I arrived
there. I rang the doorbell, but no one answered. There
were no lights on inside, but every window in the street
was dark. The freezing rain poured out of the gutters on
all sides, and I couldn't find my house keys in any of my
pockets. I hammered on the door.

"Tokki! Open the door!"

I peered through the panel of coloured glass in the
door. I thought I saw movement inside, but it was hard
to tell with all the shadows from the thrashing trees.
Someone's car alarm began to wail. I tried to open the
front window but it was locked. I tapped on the glass.
The wind continued to howl down the street; every
plant in the garden creaked and bent in surrender.

Something touched my back, and I yelled in shock.

It was one of the neighbours.

"You locked out?" she asked, voice raised against the
wind. For a second I saw long dark hair under her anorak
hood and thought she might be Tokki.

"Yes. But I think my brother is in there!"

"I didn't see him come back. But I heard the kids
didn't get let out of late night study because of the
storm! They'll probably call you. Come into ours for

now!”

I stared up at the blank windows. If Tokki was inside, he'd be in the basement, at least. Stomach in knots, I followed my neighbour across the road, into the warmth of her house, and shut the door behind me. As soon as I was inside, I tried to text Tokki, but I had no phone signal.

“No one has any signal. I suppose the mast got damaged.” My neighbour said, pouring me a cup of tea.

I stared out the window at the small house across the street.

The storm didn't let up, and I heard nothing from Tokki all night. I must have fallen asleep, because my neighbour had to shake my shoulder to inform me that one of the trees in our garden had fallen. I stumbled to the window to look. It was a tall beech. It had fallen forward, torn roots exposed, and broken the fence and the front window. The air was sodden and still when I ran out into the street. As I did so, our front door opened, swinging back and forth on its hinges. The frame must have been damaged when the tree fell. I stormed into the corridor, which was strewn with natural debris, rainwater soaking the doormat. The back door had blown open too; twigs and leaves scattered across the kitchen floor.

“Tokki! Tokki?” I shouted. I searched the ground and upper floors of the house. No one was there. I went to the basement. Tokki's bedroom door, and knocked.

Silence. I thought I heard movement.

"Tokki, I'm coming down."

It was dark, but the light turned on when I flicked the switch—evidently the power was back.

"Tokki? Sorry if I woke you."

Silence.

I stumbled to the bottom of the stairs, and the smell of earth rushed up to greet me. There was a scattering of rubble and dirt across the usually clean floor. Tokki's mattress was upturned and balanced against the wall, hiding the poster with the *Playboy* girl. Where the mattress had been was a hole. I walked over to it, staring down. It cut through the floor into the earth beyond, twisting away into the dark, a black void in the grey lino.

"Tokki?" I whispered, leaning down. The hole was pitch black like I had never seen. If you had told me that it stretched to the centre of the earth, I would have believed it. I knelt down at its edge and reached inside. The damp ends of tree roots brushed my hands. I heard a car roar down the street above, heart quickening, but I knew where safety was. Tokki knew all along. Rain soaked me through. Only one shelter can keep a storm out. I glanced around me as I dug my fingertips into the dirt. There was nothing in the room, save myself and the rabbit skull staring at me from its place on the desk.

It watched as I crawled inside the hole and disappeared.

Fig. 3 — contraception

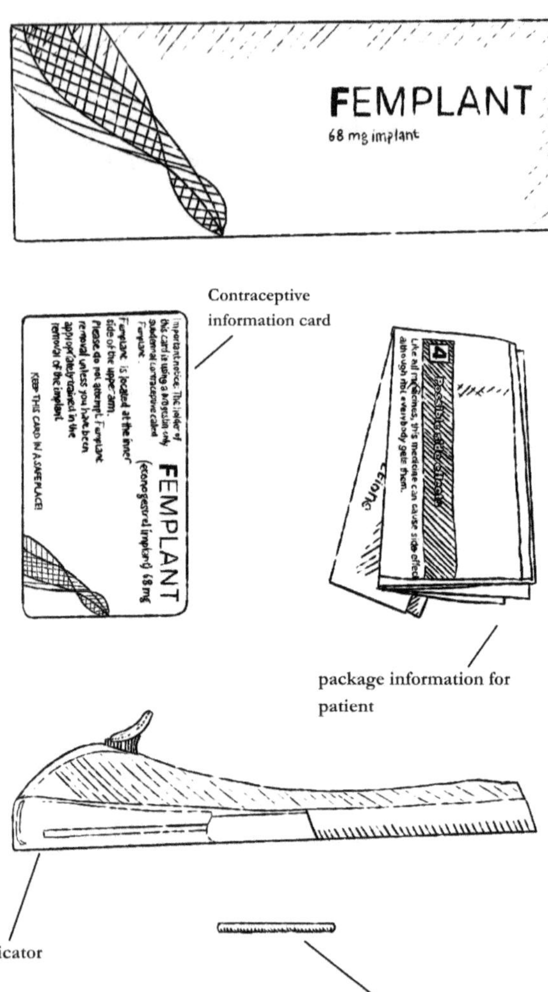

Contraceptive information card

package information for patient

applicator

contraceptive implant

Within Walls

Georgina Pearsall

"We are all haunted houses."
HD, A Tribute to Freud

Your name is Anna Williams. You live on the edge of a cul-de-sac, around which curls the river Yare, whose path detours through several fields, past four chunks of woodland, around two small lakes, under one road and across another before it delivers you to your university campus. On bright days, you like to jump the fence of your back garden and turn a half-an-hour road walk to university into an hour-and-a-half walk along the river. This avoids several landmarks you don't like, and, on most days, means you don't see another human being until you arrive.

There's a dead crow in the garden when you step outside that morning. You think it's a crow—maybe a raven? You remember what your uncle said: if it's a crow, you think "huh, wonder if that's a crow or a raven;"

if it's a raven, you think "fuck that bird is enormous."
It's strange; you don't think it was there yesterday, but
it must have been there for some time because even in
the cold weather its open stomach has started to fester,
a congregation of flies, maggots writhing. Unhappily
you acknowledge that you will have to deal with it; who
knows when someone else will notice? You scale the
fence.

Your feet are sucked into the mud when they hit the
ground on the other side of the fence, but after a second
the ground holds firm. The last few days were grey and
rainy, but today's brightness has lifted most of the water
out of the banks. The winter has pushed the foliage from
the path, and the dead leaves that made the ground slick
in the autumn have merged into the dirt. The trees are
stark and twisted, their shapes strange without their
canopies, the bark contorted into knots. Over thousands
of years, the human mind adapted to find faces in everything. You keep your eyes on the path.

You try to call your mother while you walk. Travel
used to represent a large portion of your free time, and
even though your schedule has thinned out in recent
months, the reflex to make a phone call as soon as you're
walking sticks. She left you a message last night, but now
her phone goes straight to voicemail, which is odd. She
never recorded an outgoing message, so the line rings off
then goes dead. You hang up without leaving a voicemail.
The next stretch of the river never gets a decent signal.

The river is mud-brown and murky as you ap-
proach the only sluice gate on your journey and continue

under the road. At this time of year, fish mill around
at the bottom where the water is warmest, saving their
strength, so the surface is undisturbed, eerily still.

You get to campus a few hours before your only
class of the week. You go to the library instead. It's
Friday, which means it feels a little unwelcoming, empty when it should be full. You're reading a book about
parasites your housemate Mia recommended. Ostensibly,
the book is research for a story you are writing about a
parasitical outbreak. Really, it sparked a dark, frightened
fascination and a desire to find out everything you could
about parasites. There are three more books on the
subject in your bag. You keep expecting sections to end
like stories, where the danger is eliminated or sufficiently
ridiculous that you can reject the entire conceit. Instead
they end with lists of known outbreaks, their outcomes,
and the species affected. Parasites, as it turns out, find
it easier than most pathogens to jump species barriers,
because most mammals have the same component parts.

You're about to pack up and go to class when someone from your group comes up to say hi, asks if you want
to walk over with her. Ellie, you think her name is? She's
told you at least twice. You can't ask. You ask her about
her Christmas, she returns the question, then points out
the rectangular bruise on your arm. You brush your fingers over it, a wave of nausea coming up at the memory,
and force a smile.

"Contraceptive implant. I was a little too useless to
take the pill every day." You push on it, making the strip
of plastic wiggle up and down above the pinprick fast

turning into a scar.

"Wow," she says, "did it hurt?"

You shrug. Not technically. There was a local anaesthetic, and the nurse wouldn't let you look. There was the feeling of sliding, poking through the fat, a little pinch. The ache only set in hours later, as the bruise blossomed up. You haven't quite been able to stop fiddling with it since it was put in, a little piece of rock-solid plastic moving in soft flesh. But the repeated action of taking the pill left you wandering around anxious half of the day, wondering if you'd taken it or not. In the end you carried the blister pack with you, but fishing it out of your bag six times a day to check the day marking went quickly from a comforting habit to a strange tick. It's difficult to separate instances of doing something familiar out into discrete events; every time you popped a pill from the packet and swallowed one looked exactly like every other time you did the same. You explain this to (Ellie?) and she nods sagely.

"I should probably get one, but I think me and Josh want a baby right when I graduate, y'know?"

You don't know. Getting the implant put in was traumatic, having this tiny slip removed in three years will be traumatic; the notion of birthing a baby by any method is horror beyond imagination. But you nod, and the two of you walk to class, and you try not to compare babies to parasitic larvae out loud.

Your housemate Frank recommended this module. He had been studying history with a particular bent towards folklore, and you're studying literature. The module crosses between history and literature to examine the rituals and ceremonies around death. This week you talk about *Hamlet* and Derrida and ghosts and disrupted mourning, then derail into talking about afterlives, murderers, serial killers, mass shootings, gun control, weekend plans. Then you go home. There's a voicemail message from your mum, apologising for missing your call. When you call her back the phone rings for thirty seconds then cancels itself out.

You walk home via the roads, just before four, and make it back to the house before it's completely dark. You lock the door behind you, close the blinds, and settle in for the evening. The house has four bedrooms, one downstairs and three upstairs, yours being both upstairs and the smallest. The house is from the 70s but has been through dozens of shoddy patch jobs since. The pipes bang, the floors creak, the roof tiles rattle, and the wiring doesn't make a lot of sense. Your electrician father put a shelf up when you first moved in, and the stud finder kept detecting wires and pipes in places they shouldn't have been.

You started the year with three housemates, friends you made in second year. Mia and her boyfriend Tom wanted to live together, and Frank wanted to move out of his terrible house from second year. A month before Christmas, Frank shaved his head, trashed his room, dropped out of university and bolted. You called his parents and they took the news with a weary resignation that suggested this was not the first time he'd done something like this. They live overseas, so they pay his rent while they try to arrange to collect the rest of his things. Not that he left much of value. It means you can't get someone else to fill the room. Mia and Tom broke up in week four and now compete to see who can spend the least amount of time at home. You haven't seen Mia in five days, but you haven't seen Tom in nine. They text you intermittently to ask if the other is home before they sneak back to gather changes of clothes, snacks, and shower kits and return to their encampments. In effect, you live alone, and are woefully unaccustomed to doing so. You pine for your old cat. You answer the silence with constant, uninterrupted noise: YA audiobooks, *EastEnders*, cartoon reruns, episodes of *Have I Got News For You* from 2004. Anything simplistic or familiar, so you can drift in and out of it as you bustle around doing other things. By 10 pm, you give up on anyone coming home, text them both about the crow, and go to bed.

The next day is your Saturday shift at the pub. When you get up you steel yourself to get the bird out of the garden. But it's gone, leaving no evidence behind. There isn't even a stray feather to prove it was there. Not wanting to look a gift horse in the mouth, you don't check the bin, or the other side of the fence, or the neighbour's garden. The day slips away from you, minute by minute; you're surprised when it's time to leave. You go to work at four in the afternoon, and you stay until the close.

You walk home at two in the morning. It rained all day, leaving the empty roads shining under the glow of the streetlights. The walk is a thirty-two-minute uphill trek that takes you past the university and over the river twice and you hate it. The second river crossing, the road bridge past the sluice gate, is the problem. You turn right, off the main road, and along a winding road that curls past a disused church ground and an outpatient hospital that has its lights on all night. In the daytime it's barely sinister, but in the dark the muffled glow from the windows refracts against the church and throws odd shadows. Once those fall out of sight, owing to another bend in the road, you walk out onto the traffic bridge. The road is clean and deserted. There are houses ahead of you, but they're distant and you're short-sighted. The land that separates them from everything behind you might have been farmland ten years ago, but econom-ic shifts have turned it into common land, not worth growing on. Sometimes the farmers graze animals there, but in the dark it's impossible to say if there's anything in the fields. If Frank's past lectures about folklore are to be believed, it's a bad idea to look across the fields at night anyway. They stretch far enough that you can't see the edges. Crossing the bridge is a moment of perfect isolation. Tall trees cocoon you, but they're spindly and bare, and they drop long shadows over the fields where they block the streetlights.

The bridge itself is hushed, but the river is loud underfoot. You listen for your footsteps, but they're swallowed by the wind and the water. It rained all night and most of the day, and the banks are swollen, sending water plummeting over the sluice, and the noise echoes beneath the bridge. It pounds in your ears like rushing blood. The path is narrow, which forces you close to the flimsy railing that separates you from a six-foot drop into the river.

The rain is gone, but the wind remains. It rattles the railing and howls as it skates under the bridge. The smell of the river is everywhere, damp and rot and rain. When you look down through the railing the river is glowing, ethereal, as the moon pours light into it. The concrete feels precarious. The shadows over the fields shift in the wind, flickering, then they start to disappear. You look up at the road. Ahead of you the streetlights go out sequentially. It starts at the furthest point of your vision, half a mile up, curving around the bend in the road, then continues up the road towards you until the final street-light above your head burns out with a crackle. You bark out half a nervous laugh. The wind screams through the railings. You walk faster.

Norfolk has the country's highest concentration of medieval churches. You wonder why they kept on building churches, one after the other. What were they praying for?

From the bridge you turn left, re-joining with the river as it stretches to the housing estate. You move away from it behind the walls, but it cuts up most of the city.

You're never far away from it, and sometimes you come upon it unexpectedly. The river is supposed to be haunted, but in the manner of all the local legends that pass from the locals to the students, the details are muddy at best. Rivers make sense as places that might be haunted. People must have died in or around the Yare, and rivers are a strange kind of alive themselves, moving and churning and full of algae and bacteria respiring under the surface, pushing air out, sucking air in. A body of water. A body dumped into water will, as a part of decomposition, be filled with carbon dioxide by the bacteria digesting it from the inside out, causing it eventually to rise to the surface. This is why bodies dumped in water by professionals are well-weighted.

The sensation lingers on your skin. Haunted. You wrote all of the feelings down for three weeks, until the journal disappeared, and the feeling that someone was onto you made you edgy. There's a church around the corner from your house. The bell, pre-recorded and just slightly out of tune, pipes out from the top of the bell tower. The church itself is seldom used for actual prayer, more of a village hall, and the bell could be announcing anything, you suppose. You itch for the journal. You don't buy a new one.

You got your first pet at ten, a black-and-white cat with white paws, a true witch's cat. You named him Hades and you loved him more than anything in the entire world. He slept on the floor beside your bed, standing vigil to keep you safe. When you were thirteen, Hades started to climb onto your bedside table and cry. He would sit there and screech into the blackness beyond your bedroom door. Nothing could console him; you woke up whenever he started and you sat up in bed with your back to the wall as Hades cried into the darkness and you stared out at nothing with him until morning.

When you were fourteen Hades left your bedside

to prowl downstairs overnight, creating odd clattering noises as he pounced at dust and disturbed the furniture. It was an old house and the pipes creaked, the floors groaned, the roof tiles rattled. You still slept with your door open, because you were afraid that the walls would collapse around you and you would be trapped, shaking at the door handle as it held stiff. You practised climbing from your bedroom window, over the porch roof, the safe drop to the ground. Your window faced a line of houses that stared back at you when you peered out, and there was a shadow on your bedroom wall you could never place. No, not a shadow; a shadow is the absence of light. This was a patch of light that appeared on the wall every night, unprovoked, and it didn't dissipate when you drew the curtain. You know, rationally, that the human mind is trained to find human faces and silhouettes in everything. But you don't know where the light came from.

Hades has been dead for three years. You arrive home to find a power outage. You know the bill is paid; you're the one who pays it. It's gone two, the letting agency stops answering their phones at six, and it's too late to call your mother. Fresh from the cold the central heating makes you sweat. Down the road there's a cat screeching. At what? There are no cars, no pedestrians other than you. You double check the door and look for the fuse box. A door creaks upstairs.

"Mia?" Silence. "Tom?"

Anywhere with a castle has seen a few executions. A 2016 survey of very questionable origin calls Norwich the most haunted city in the UK. You can find three murders in the last fifty years in your district, but none of them have a specific enough address attached for you to figure out where exactly. Norwich Castle used to gibbet prisoners, like a chained hanging, suspending people from the walls until they died of exposure.

No one answers. The fuse box is in one of the cupboards, either the weird one behind the fridge or the spider-filled menace under the stairs. It takes you a good minute to find the torch button on your phone. But you find the fuse box and flip the switches back into place, and all of the lights come on. So someone was home today, at least long enough to leave all of the lights on. Upstairs, jolted into life, Tom's clock radio starts playing the evening news. The tumble dryer resumes its cycle. The house is messy, but otherwise undisturbed. There's washing up still in the sink and the floors need sweeping, but these problems are deferred until morning. Mia leaves half-drunk mugs of tea around until she runs out of mugs, washes them, and starts over. By your estimates she's halfway through. Tom's coat is on the sofa, and you're pretty sure it was his leather jacket yesterday, so he's been in at one time or another. You make a quick circuit of the house, turning off the lights and darting from the room, trying to get out before all the light is gone. Upstairs the doors are wide open, giving a gaping view of Tom and Mia's unmade, empty beds. You steal into Tom's room and switch the radio off at the plug, throwing the house back into quiet, save for the regular clanking of jeans in the tumble dryer. You shut yourself in your room.

You keep meaning to call the letting agency, because the seal has blown in your bedroom window. At first it just created a draught that made you crank up the heating, fluttered papers on your desk if the blind was up. But now the blind is never raised. Now the weather has started to turn truly wintry, the wind howls when it hits the perished rubber. You sleep poorly.

The next day you're reluctant to go out. It's raining again, for one, and bitterly cold. Plus it's Sunday, so there's no class, no work. And there was that thing with the streetlights. You're not acknowledging the thing with the streetlights. It was late, you were tired, it could have been any level of electrical fault. You Google around to see if any of the local news sites have reported the outage. You check the council website to see if streetlights in this area automatically switch off to save energy at night. No luck.

Looking around the house you struggle to remember the last time you spent a full day at home. The space feels alien. You gather up Mia's mugs, hang Tom's coat. Someone has opened Frank's door, so you shut it. You wash, dry, and put away the dishes, even if half of the putting away is guesswork. You vacuum, and mop, and dust, and polish. You tidy your room down to putting all of the books on your desk at right angles. You make dinner rather than eating out for the first time in a week. There was a leak under the floor over Christmas. The letting agency sent a plumber last week, who stripped the face from the boiler and tweaked dials, disconnected and reconnected pipes, removed the panel hiding the pipes underneath the sink and tightened joints while you watched from the doorway. The leak stopped and the boiler stopped catapulting between maximum and minimum pressure with no apparent pattern. The floor is raised and bubbled, some part of the underlay swollen beyond the point of shrinking back to size, and the panels irreversibly misshapen. The landlord told you they would replace it over the summer, after you move out. The floorboards are still wet. They still squelch and shift under your feet, press up and down like skin stretched over fat, water pressing out from between the cracks. It never moves in the same place, like rot spreading unseen. You scratch your arm, scrape your fingernails against the bruise and feel the plastic matchstick wiggle. You can't shut the door anymore, the wood scrapes against the lino. You begin to dislike the kitchen. The window is too big, too reflective; it makes the room look distorted and lets too much of the outside in. You shut the blind and eat in the newly tidied living room.

The church bells ring again at about seven thirty for no discernible reason. You peek out of a window at the front of the house, sneaking into Frank's room to do so, and fancy you can see the top of the church. The original bell was taken out years ago. You used to volunteer with a children's reading group on a Sunday afternoon, so you know the bell is a fake, but you're looking at it like you expect to see it twitch. Frank's books are still spread over his bed. You recall some snatch of conversation from the few weeks you were all together before everything happened. Frank liked to say that the best advice you can get from folklore worldwide is that first, you don't have to believe in something to not want to piss it off, and second, the best thing you can do to avoid pissing something off is not look. You let the blind drop closed.

You watch TV for a while, fall asleep on the sofa for a while longer. Mia wakes you at about nine thirty, barrelling through the door in her usual manner and calling your name. You jerk awake and try to re-acclimatise, but Mia flicks the light on before your eyes have time to adjust. The room feels smaller. She dumps a bag on the floor, talking even as she disappears into the kitchen and reappears with glasses, produces a bottle of chardonnay and flops onto the sofa in front of the window.

"I am so glad you're here, by the way, God. I feel like I haven't been home in weeks."

One week, actually. Mia scrubs her hands over her face. She's been crying. She's on the brink of bursting, staring at you, waiting for some kind of permission. It's dark now; it wasn't when you fell asleep. The living room has this big window that overlooks the garden, fitted with a tatty roller blind. She pours you each a glass of wine and forces the cup into your hands. You sip, casting an eye back over the room. You're about to ask how she is, really, but then:

"Did you move those books?"

"What?" she asks, following your line of sight to the stack of books spread over the TV cabinet. "I don't know, does it matter?"

"No, they're fine wherever, just, did you move

them?"

"Anna, more pressing issues at hand."

"Yeah. Sorry. Of course. How are you?"

She starts talking about Tom, and how he's the worst person in the entire world, and about Frank, and how she felt a stronger connection with him anyway but he left, and over her right shoulder there's a full moon glinting against the glass. And don't people always leave? There's something about a pregnancy scare and how polyamory is really complicated, and the glass in that window is strange, because it turns completely reflective when it's dark outside. You're not down here much after dark anyway but you draw the blind if you are, would have already if you hadn't fallen asleep. When were you last in the living room in the evening? You sip your wine and make some kind of assenting noise to Mia, who continues, something about an ex coming to town, something about Frank's disappearance.

"Are you listening to me?"

"Yeah of course I am, sorry, do you mind if I just close the blind though?"

"What?"

Actually, who opened the blind in the first place? The back garden is north facing and practically pressed against the fence, you don't get any light during the day. You didn't open it when you cleaned this morning. You realise that Mia was still talking and she's started crying again. You start to apologise, but it's too late. She calls you weird and insensitive and storms out, slamming the front door. You close the blind, but not before you catch sight of something shifting behind you in the flash of reflection. You turn slowly, pointedly not looking at the wall opposite the window, and you go upstairs and shut yourself in your room. Then shutting the door feels like a bad idea, so you open it again. Then that feels too exposed, so you settle for pushing it until it's ajar. Your childhood fear of entrapment, put living into the tomb, lingers, but it mingles with your adulthood fear of pursuit and both sit leaden in your bowel. The house feels small. Suffocating. Your lungs swell inside your thorax, like your ribcage can't contain them. Frank's history books and Mia's medical texts brush up against each other; you think about locked-in syndrome and about immurement, the practice of entombing a living person. Tom's language-student fascination with Latin lingers on the outskirts, "murus" for wall, prefix "in." "Within walls."

In the natural order of entropy, the more you try to organise your space, the faster it slides into chaos. By the next day the house has started to slip back towards mess, which is confusing until you hear Tom bustling around upstairs. He's quiet, unlike Mia, not always certain to wake you when he comes in. You go up to say hi, lingering in his doorway. He's unpacking a bag, emptying clothes into his laundry basket and gathering clean clothes from the wardrobe. He has the radio on, the news talking about a cold front coming in.

"Hey. Might be snow," Tom says, when he looks up and sees you standing there. "Just getting some more appropriate clothes."

You nod. "How's it going?"

"Yeah. Been crashing with a mate. You know, getting high, avoiding responsibilities. Life as usual. You?"

"Fine. I barely have class this semester anyway. Mia came home last night, pretty briefly. I know you'll be heartbroken to have missed her."

Tom grimaces, folding a shirt. You smile.

"She was asking about Frank, actually. And I was wondering if he gave his key back when he left? Seems weird to think of it just floating around out there. I mean, I never have any idea who's been home."

"You're so paranoid," he laughs, "if I tell you something, will you keep it a secret? He doesn't want Mia to know, or his parents."

"Sure? What is it?"

He takes out his phone, flips through a few screens. Frank peers out at you, stood in front of the Rijksmuseum in a winter coat, giving you a thumbs up.

"He's been travelling," Tom explains, flicking back a screen so you can see a few messages and the time-stamp on the picture. Yesterday. "His parents are crazy, apparently, and he didn't like the house so he just bounced."

"Why didn't you tell me?"

He looks at you a little sheepishly, shrugs. "Don't know, really. Thought you might tell Mia. Frank asked me not to tell her, then I just knew exactly how the conversation would go—you know how dramatic she is—so I just... yeah. But Frank is like, gone, but safe, so don't worry, okay?"

"Yeah. Thanks for letting me know."

You chat while he finishes packing, or he chats, and you stand mostly listening. So it has just been you and Mia and Tom in and out of the house. It ought to be reassuring.

Tom finishes packing and heads back out. You walk him to the door. The sky is threatening overhead, grey and churning. He tells you to be careful.

"I mean, because of the snow," he explains.

"Oh. Of course. You too. I'll see you around."

With Tom gone you dawdle around and note the amount of chaos he's managed to create. Maybe he stayed the night, came in after you were asleep, didn't wake you in that time. You retreat to your room and find it out of order. You were barely here. You re-tidy the space. You think about going out for a while, walking around, maybe pottering down to the shops to restock a little. You don't have to do so often; Mia and Tom keep so little in the house that you have more freezer, fridge, and cupboard space than you could fill alone. You're disaster prepared, with bottled water and cans and frozen food.

You sit in the kitchen for a while watching Netflix on your laptop, until you become aware of a persistent dripping sound. You stand up and turn around, ready to tighten the tap, but there isn't any water visible, just the sound, dripping on. You tighten the taps. You mute your laptop to check the noise isn't coming from there. The drip continues. You take your laptop and you go back upstairs, and you stay there until night.

It's soft at first, crackling. Like plastic, not like fire.

The noise is not sinister. The heating went off four hours ago, and outside of your bed it's maybe sixteen degrees.

You check your phone. It is three in the morning. Your alarm will go off in five hours. You have a meeting to go to.

You reach an arm out of the covers and turn up your laptop, an old episode of *Waterloo Road*. The noise seems quieter, but the music stings are unbearable at this volume. You swap to an old episode of *Mock The Week*, but then the laugh track judders around the room. You roll onto your other side. Go to sleep. It's nothing. It's always nothing. It'll be the window, the wind, the pipes, the house is weird and echoey. There's a crackle, followed by a low rumble, and it sounds like it's coming from downstairs. Your laptop screen times out and the room is back to darkness. You crawl out of bed and shiver your way out of the room. The bulb in the hall blew a few months ago, and you live alone, so it hasn't been replaced yet. You walk downstairs slowly, the rattle—definitely the kitchen—turns into a low hiss. As your foot touches the floor the boiler gives a final bang, like something thumping on the inside of the casing, then stops. The lights flicker out. For a few minutes it creaks and ticks, cooling down, like a final death rattle. You make a noise back, half-groan half-sob, and retreat upstairs.

This time you shut the door tight.

There has to be something making you feel like this.

The next morning when you sit up, still wrapped in your covers, your stuffed bear is sitting upright on the desk at the end of the room. You think you went to sleep with it in bed with you, you do so every night, but in light of that you can't separate out the memory of doing so last night specifically. You get dressed as quickly as possible in the cold, and you take your phone downstairs. The emergency plumber tells you in Norfolk twang that he can't get out in the snow, which makes you look outside for the first time in eighteen hours. The door sticks when you open it, crunching over a foot and a half of snow. Paul promises you'll be the first on his list when the roads clear up, but the city is half-buried, the rivers starting to freeze for the first time in years. You hang up and find yourself standing in the kitchen, looking out of the back door at the garden, where there is a dead crow in the middle of the lawn, lying on the unspoiled snow. Its stomach is open, a perfect patch of spilling red, but nothing is there to bother at the wound. Hades used to catch birds, drag their guts out, scatter feathers. There are no footprints around the corpse. Its surroundings are clean.

Your phone rings in your hand, startling. Your mother at last.

"Hi, Mum."

"Hi, sweetpea. Look I can't stay on the phone long. I've been calling all week—your Uncle Robert died. He had a stroke on Friday. Totally blindsided all of us. They resuscitated him, kept him on support over the weekend, but I don't think he was really there. Took him off last night. Anna? Are you there?"

"I—yes, Mum, I'm here. That's awful. Are you okay?"

"Yes, yes, more worried about his kids. But I have to be off; we're supposed to go and pick up the death certificate so we can get started on the funeral. Are you alright?"

You survey the kitchen. The swollen floor. The leaking tap. The snow creeping over the threshold.

"Yeah. Fine, Mum. You should get on."

"Alright. Talk soon."

She hangs up. A stroke. Out of nowhere. Robert was healthy, then he was a corpse propped up by life support, then he was gone. You scratch your arm. You notice something in the sink. There's an orange sitting in the plug hole. Someone, Mia, has sliced a line in the skin and sewn it back together. A practice suture. You pick it up and run your finger down the wound. The edges have started to dry and wrinkle. Pull away from the stitching.

Your implant throbs. When you poke at it, it's hot and red. You scratch at it, nails blunt against the skin. It's infected. Or it's moved. You wrestle the little card out of your wallet. You're supposed to go to A&E right away, but the roads are all blocked. The doctor said there might be some movement, but it's stinging, it's poison, what if it's infected? A little parasite, and you let them put it in, shove it past all of the barriers.

You become aware all at once that you occupy a human body. You prefer to think of yourself as mechanical, like wires and metal. Solid. Impersonal. Like someone could take you apart and put you back together, nothing lost. You may prefer to think of yourself as soul, memories and consciousness and divine.

You walk upstairs. Ethylene vinyl-acetate copolymer, one point five inches, delivering a constant feed of hormones. You press on it, hard. It moves up and down. You press harder. Has it moved? Where did it start?

You're sweating. Action of adrenaline from the adrenal glands nestled above your kidneys. Flooding your endocrine system, slower but more universal than a nervous reaction. Longer lasting. You are all soft and squishy parts, governed by chemical reactions that will fail if they're off by a milligram. You take a safety razor out of the bathroom and crush it on your desk with the spine of Mia's textbook. You push the pieces apart, spreading them out. The blades are thin and narrow, but they're sharp. You pick one out with your fingernails.

You are churning bile and dying cells. Tubes and nodes and a million tiny things you can't see. Everything inside you is too big and too small at once. More bacterial cells than human. You wipe your arm with alcohol gel from your desk drawer. It's cold against the hot skin.

Have you ever seen a wound you couldn't imagine healing?

There are seven types of basic medical suture, appropriate to different purposes. This would likely require a subcuticular, a stitch that pulls together the second layer of skin rather than the first, to create less of a scar.

You dig the thin blade into your arm and drag it down fast, hard. You cut your fingertips in the process, letting go of the blade, leaving it sticking out of the arm. You press fingers inside, pinching out the blade. You dig back in for the implant, feeling the movement of tissues, muscle fibres, leaking capillaries. From the window you can see the river, stopped dead in its tracks. The pain is so delayed, adrenaline-dulled, that it feels alien. Like a loading screen is separating you from your body. You grip the end of the strip and pull it free.

On the desk in front of you it writhes.

Fig. 4 — egg timer
chicken-shaped case
double spiral spring
gear top plate
metal shell
inner gear
bell pivot arm
machine screws
spring

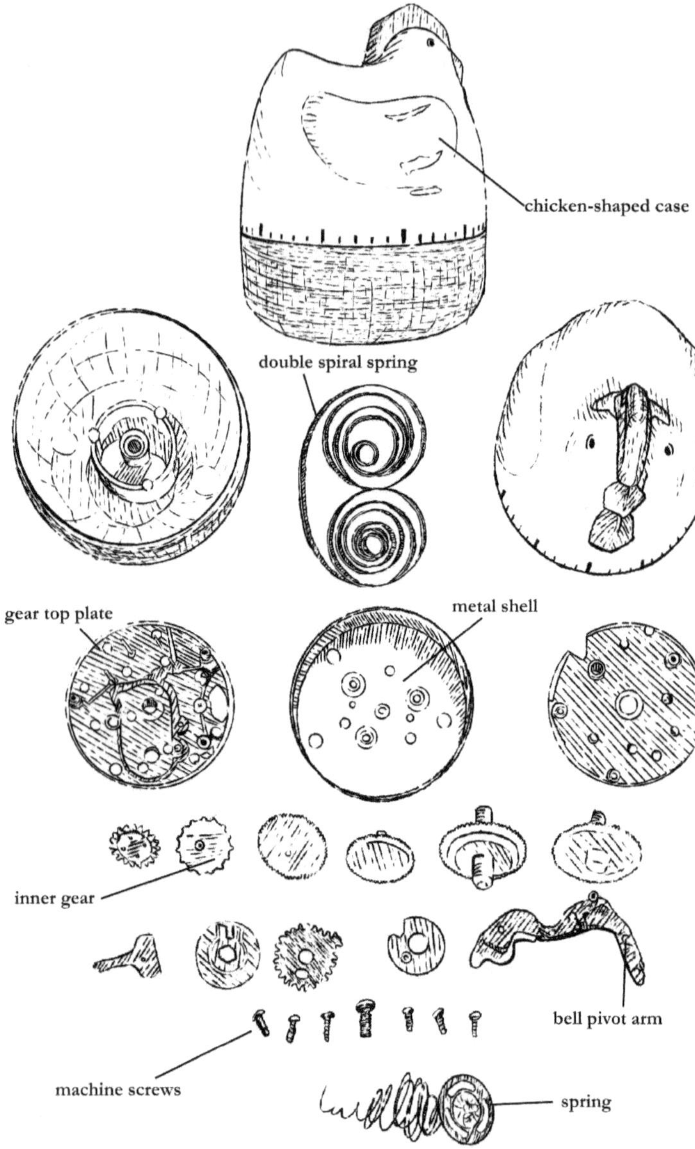

Not a River

Harry Menear

HP LOVECRAFT, "THE NIGHTMARE LAKE"

WHERE'S EMILY?
December frost clots the grass. Thin, wet sunlight shines through the skeletal beech trees and lies in doubloons and Yellow King gold on the lawn. The aga sighs as Classic FM rattles out Vivaldi's "Spring" for the third time this morning. Emily is probably in the living room, playing seriously with chessmen and the Sky remote. Steam rises from the coffee pot. Helen reaches for the cup, the sugar, the cream. She watches as silken tendrils of white writhe and diffuse into a gentle, comforting brownness. She rests the tip of her chin on her hand and stares into the space

between the kettle and a novelty Kath Kidson egg timer in the shape of a chicken. Vivaldi plays on, his enthusiasm undimmed by the repeat performance. Helen doesn't hear it. She's thinking about the duck pond.

Ducks don't land on it.

They'd put fish in it that September, when the moving vans had migrated away and the boxes had been unpacked, when the weather was still warm and the only thing in the garden that wasn't achingly picturesque at sunset—with a nice glass of chablis—was that scrap of deep green water.

The fish were polished bronze and tamarin gold— God knows they were expensive enough. A friend of a friend had sent Helen to Chinatown, to a shop with dim, algae-frosted glass and tepid air. The sign out front screamed: *MAKE YOUR LIFE MORE IMPRESSIVE.* Helen still thinks about it sometimes.

The receipt had been handwritten, and her crisp twenties were held up to the light just long enough for it to be insulting. She'd tried not to touch anything, but the smell still clung to her coat: fish food musk and brackish water.

The fish had arrived the following Monday: large men carrying plastic chests full of treasure. Emily was delighted. These were not the mismatched, swollen fairground goldfish that tarnish after a long weekend; they were fat, serene baubles, like Enlightenment kings. They drifted in the green water, catching flecks of food, catching the light. They were all dead in a week—white bellies clouded with pond scum, obscene on a cold Monday morning. Emily was late for school, so Helen left them there all day and by the time she got back, had a cup of tea, and got the old shrimping net from the potting shed, birds had ripped the glittering things apart. They lay on the bank. Half-open. Still.

Helen's foot taps the heated flagstones. The kitchen is too warm for slippers. The thought shifts, deep down, flicking a golden fin: *Where's Emily?* Sound doesn't carry well across inch-thick carpet, through renewably-sourced oak doors. Helen wonders about the chances of Emily accidentally ordering pay-per-view movies by pressing the most colourful buttons on the remote. The duck pond sits uncomfortably behind her, like the tag on a cheap shirt—digging away at the top of her spine.

Ducks don't land on it.

The frogs appeared overnight—out of nowhere, out of season. There was no frogspawn; a thousand virgin births turned the grass a new shade of green. She'd shouted and shooed and the wriggling mass had watched with a thousand cold wet eyes until Emily waddled out the back door, holding a plush Kermit by the flipper, laughing. The wriggling, hopping mass fell quiet. Yellow, bulging, glistening eyes fixed upon Her, breath held tighter than the yawning, silent chasm before the orchestra's first note. Helen led Emily back inside by a freckled hand in case she ruined her new dress in the dirt. Once more, the mass began to wriggle.

At night they threw themselves through the cat flap; fragile October light fell every morning on a kitchen floor that moved. And when Helen boarded the hole in the door, they still threw themselves against the cheap plywood. They sang baritone sonatas, keeping her awake until dawn. Emily was sent to stay with her aunt in the third week of the siege.

There was a small piece in the local news. The photographer, a thin man in a windbreaker with cigarette holes in his sleeves and a pencil mustache worked his camera in silence. He left the tea Helen made him half-finished and promised to send along a copy of the article. She kept the clipping in the study drawer marked "*misc.*"

Boys in flannel shorts with waterfalls of snot on their upper lips stopped to gawk over the fence. They stuffed twitching handfuls of legs and eyes and taupe bodies into their rucksacks. They cycled home, fishtailing tires through the first November frost. The best half term ever.

A puzzled ecologist took some of the frogs away with her, then asked if she could take some samples from the duck pond. She hasn't been back, but the frogs are gone. Helen was almost used to the constant croaking that lapped around the house like waves against a wooden hull. She filled her sleep playlist with the sounds of deepest jungle in the treacle night and dreamed of steel bands around her lungs, her stomach, her heart. Emily came home wearing bright yellow gumboots her aunt bought for her—even though Christmas was weeks away.

Helen refills her coffee cup—cream, two sugars, stir. On the side of the cup, a sad bulldog watches her, draped in the Union Flag. She knows it's only the Union Jack when flown at sea—*Jeopardy*, three nights ago on the channel that plays American TV two decades out of sync.

What is the Union Flag? Where's Emily?

In mid-November, the radio stopped picking up Classic FM for a while. Helen assumed it was some experimental prelude to "The Water Babies" by Frederick Rosse, but the sounds of breathing, of waves unbroken in deep, cold water never gave way to woodwinds and the comfort of a brass section. Low timpani and hollow voices filled the house with whispers. Helen had sat through several of Classic FM's "phases" before, and might have been willing to forgive them for assigning the mutterings of forgotten gods in the dark quite so much airtime, if the noise had stopped when she switched off the radio. So, she and Emily danced around the kitchen with KISS FM turned up almost loud enough for a whole week before Helen realised the noise had stopped. She couldn't remember what the voices said, but she could no longer stand to listen to Frederick Rosse in the bath, or anything by Tears for Fears for that matter.

The radio vibrates gently on the windowsill as the brass section comes in. Helen reaches for a pen and the Times Cryptic. All the clues but one have been answered, though she can't remember filling it in, or owning a pen that writes in deep, liver red, or her handwriting being so beautiful. *Seven down, 6, 5. Clue: Bronte dresses are in fashion, so She ---*

Where's Emily? Helen stares at the page, lips pursed. She tuts. An ambulance wails in the next street.

Early December. Every house tinselled up and sprouted fairies on dead pines. Carollers roamed the streets in packs, selling holy nights and jingling bells for charity or the church roof. The duck pond glowed, spitting faerie fire and sprouted purple bulrushes that swayed as they sang gospel call and response over the garden fence. It was a shame about the St. Peter Mancroft church roof repair fundraising committee (Caroling with Christ). They stood for six days at the garden fence, singing to the reeds, swaying with them like lovers. They drank snow and sucked worms from the earth. And lo, did they waste away, dying in twos and threes, rejecting Emily's half-hearted attempts to feed them chocolate digestives through a hole in the fence. On the seventh day, the good Father Graham rested, face down in the duck pond. He must have climbed over in the night, the police agreed. He was a large man, so he stayed there all afternoon, thin light rolling like lemon curd around his sodden collar, as shadows reached for his blue lips, for his smile—beatitude, be good, or Santa won't be coming down the chimney. Then the police came back with a bigger net, and a hedge trimmer for the bulrushes.

The coffee is cold, and Helen moves to refill the kettle. A flock of ducks trails through the eggshell December sky that stretches from the top of the fence to forever without a hint of cloud. Helen wonders whether she can serve Chicken Parma for a third night in a row without Emily throwing some sort of tantrum.

The neighbours had begun complaining around Christmas. This was a *good* area. *Respectable*, they clucked. There were standards. They had seen the gentlemen callers coming. And going. At all hours and, well, it just wasn't proper was it? Helen tried to explain, as firmly as she could, that the Cold-eyed men with iridescent skin and expensive suits were more than welcome to call during business hours. It was her house after all. She had slammed the door on the neighbours and brewed her morning coffee in a huff. The *nerve*.

Unfortunately, she conceded—quietly and to herself—they had a point. The cold-eyed men came and went as they pleased—at breakfast, right in the middle of lunch, in the wee hours when Helen crept into the kitchen for just one last slice of nettle-wrapped yarg and a cold mince pie and caught them by the glow of the fridge, emptying more and more of the struggling sacks they carried into the churning green water of the duck pond. Above it seemed to squirm an aurora of living, ice cold neon that danced in a dizzying tapestry, a chorus line of purple and green above the rotting bullrushes. It grew brighter with the contents of each sack. Emily had been worried that they wouldn't be able to see the fireworks come New Year's.

Where's Emily?

Helen tuts again, putting the crossword away. Rustling the paper indignantly as she folds and refolds it; the pages have come out of order and refuse to lie back down again in the meek, pristine posture they'd adopted on the front step this morning. She stares into the space between the kettle and something unknowable with too many eyes, frozen in the process of climbing back into the fridge. Watching her. It looks nervous, she thinks. Guilty. The pen remains in her hand, tapping against the table. *Tap tap tap tap.* The thing with too many eyes and teeth and not enough respect for how one should behave when traveling through euclidean space resumes its slow progress into the folding space between infinity and a pint of semi-skimmed. *Tap tap... Tap.* Helen purses her lips. Maybe tonight she'll go down to the duck pond, with a candle and her nightdress at full sail, and give it a piece of her mind. Enough is enough. Steam rises from the coffee pot. Helen refills her cup and watches the bulldog. It doesn't look much like a bulldog any more; the design on the flag is more complex; skulls and teeth and deep green eyes are more prominent now. Something big bumps against the cat flap. The door creaks. *Where's Emily?*

Helen sighs and hopes that Emily doesn't swallow any of the chessmen.

Fig. 5 — orange
oil sacs
albedo
segment
flavedo
pith
peel
pip
juice vesicles

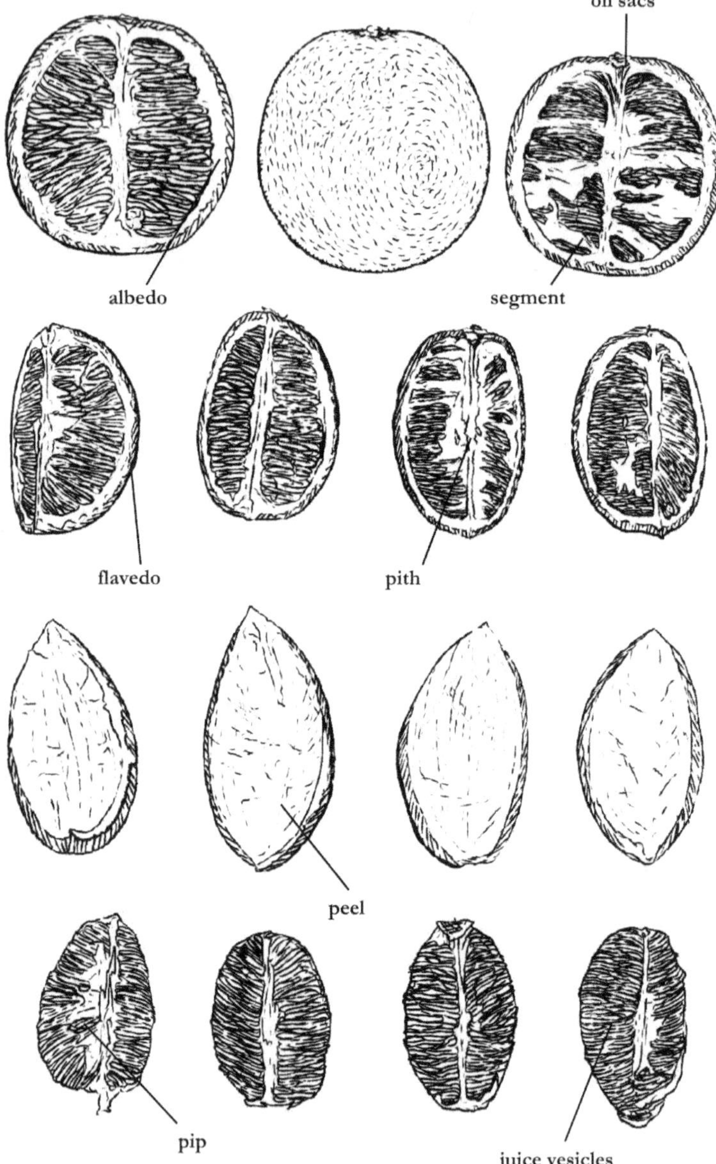

Spiderling

Shannon Lewis

H E WOKE UP WITH AN EARACHE. OR HE woke up because of an earache. As he sat there rubbing the right side of his head with his palm, the pain melted away. It wasn't even pain, per se, more like pressure. A tiny silver ball pressed against his eardrum. There was no reason rubbing the outside of his ear should have worked to alleviate anything. He wondered if it hadn't been some vestigial dream pain. He rarely remembered his dreams.

The light spilling in around the edges of his blackout curtains was cold and grey. He wondered what time it was. As soon as his fingers wrapped around his phone, it began to vibrate, accompanied by a high tinkling noise. He swiped at the screen until it stopped.

The amount of time he had between his alarm going off and when he had to leave the house for work was exactly 35 minutes—just enough time to jump in the shower, comb his hair, and eat an orange. That was enough to get him through to mid-morning, when he made himself toast in the communal kitchen. Once, a couple months ago, he broke routine and made himself a cup of coffee to enjoy alongside the fruit. Huge mistake. He spent his entire commute in nose-to-nose traffic with a bursting bladder.

Today, everything felt off-kilter, likely because he woke up right before his alarm. The shower seemed to take longer than usual to heat up and he ended up rushing out the door with one shoe untied. As he locked up behind him, he noticed a spider web blossoming in the upper-right corner of the door frame. A shudder passed through him. So it was that season again. There was no spider that he could see, but the web hung there, bold and gossamer.

As he drove down the main stretch of highway, he kept thinking about the web. Back when he had housemates, they tore them down for him. They moved out a while ago, but he still hadn't found any replacements. His job paid well enough that he could easily cover rent and utilities on his own. Maybe he'd just reached that age.

He wished he had reached up and shaken it loose himself. Now he was going to have to come home to it at night, when he was much less in the mood. Even as he thought this, he knew he was being unrealistic. The prospect of the spider crawling down from some hidden corner onto his hand was enough to make his skin crawl even here, in the car, several miles from the offending location. He read somewhere once that people who were scared of spiders were more likely to see them, which felt deeply unfair. He spent the rest of the car ride gripping the steering wheel, knuckles bone white.

Work was no more or less hectic than usual. His mid-morning toast came from the bread at the end of the packet, so it was dry and he spent the rest of the day feeling like he had something lodged in his throat. Once, when he tilted his head to face a colleague, his hair brushed the back of his neck and he jumped, the sudden brush of tiny hairs sending shivers down his spine. He'd have to go to the barber this weekend.

By the time he got home, he was drained. It was only after he'd made himself dinner, a frozen meal thrown in the oven, brushed his teeth, and picked tomorrow's outfit, after he'd gotten snug in bed, enjoying the cool silk of his sheets pressed against his bare legs, that he remembered the web. Damn it. He took a slow breath, conceptualising a plan of action. His porch light was broken, so he couldn't go now anyway—he wouldn't be able to find it in the dark. Besides, he was warm in bed and it was cold outside and there was no reason he couldn't figure it out tomorrow. The unease of a spider lurking somewhere nearby would have to wait.

He slept terribly that night. He woke up intermittently, never for very long, but always feeling dreadfully uncomfortable. The covers were too hot, tangling no matter which way he turned. The air was stale, unbreathable. He could have reached out and opened the window, but that seemed impossible in his half-conscious state. The dreams were the worst of it. He couldn't remember them exactly, but images kept flashing in his head: something crooked, spools of something else, a raking sensation. All he could muster in those moments was a vague certainty that this was related to the throbbing pain that emanated from his right ear.

When his alarm went off the next morning, he had no memory of any of this. Only the sandy feeling in his eyes of having not slept very well. He turned his alarm off and rolled back in bed, promising himself he would get up and started in just two minutes. He woke up again fifteen minutes later, heart pounding.

He skipped the shower and went straight to breakfast. He had learned long ago that for him to be functional for the workday, eating trumped hygiene. He sat at the kitchen table peeling his orange, dazed. There was a rustle by the window followed by a thump. He turned to see a fuzzy calico cat meowing mournfully at him. He smiled and unlatched the window to let Athena in. Athena hopped off the sill onto his lap and immediately began purring.

She probably hated the cold weather, because he started closing the window earlier and earlier in the day and she couldn't get in whenever she pleased. He scratched the crook right where the back of her ear met her head and murmured, "Alright, but I don't have very long." The cat's owner remained a mystery, but there was something soothing in her methodical hum. The morning took on a slow creamy quality, like something filmed underwater. Maybe he should get a cat of his own.

Lazily, he flipped his phone screen to check the time. Reality crashed back in on him. He was already late, and his orange half eaten.

He stood up with a jolt, toppling Athena onto the ground. She gave a disgruntled cry but he was too busy scrambling for his coat, scarf, and car keys to feel bad. He didn't have time to coax her back outside, so he left the window unlatched. The front door clattered opened under his sweaty palms and he burst across the threshold like a runner at the end of a race. When he felt something sinewy across his face, he realised he had run straight into the spider web, which had grown downwards through the night. A panic overtook him as he scrambled to scratch the offending material off, pricks of pale motion erupting over his face. He imagined the feeling of toothpick legs shimmying up his arms and had to stifle a scream. Having scraped the stuff off him, he gave himself a thorough pat-down, checking for the spider. Once sure he was clear, he looked around to see if it was dangling in some corner, watching with macabre delight. But it was nowhere. He grunted. It had to be somewhere. Webs didn't just appear.

When he got into his car, still panting, he noticed a large pink scratch across his forehead. He sighed, steadying his breathing. The scarf around his neck was starting to make him feel too hot. It was restrictive, wrapping around and around him like a trap. A flash of the Discovery Channel stabbed his brain. A wolf spider sticking its plush fangs into a still-wriggling silk sack. The orange half churned in his stomach.

Five separate people at the office asked him what happened to his head. The lie that he had bumped it against the door frame seemed mundane enough to keep further questions at bay. He made himself an extra slice of toast that morning, to make up for the incomplete orange, but found he couldn't bring himself to eat any of it. It felt like concrete on his tongue.

When he headed home that night, he was starving and exhausted. Even in that state, he reminded himself to keep an eye out on his way into the house. The parts of the web in the upper corner that he had destroyed had been rebuilt, with an additional compartment sprawling over his broken porch light. The arachnid was nowhere to be seen.

His house was freezing inside. Athena was long gone, but the window had remained open, letting autumnal air pour in. He closed the latch and turned up the heating, figuring he deserved it, if just for one night. He got to work on dinner, sticking a frozen lasagna into the oven. As he waited for it to cook, he figured now was as good a time as any to finally crack open the bottle of wine his housemates had given him as a moving out present. It was odd, now that he thought of it, that they gave him the present when he was the one staying put.

He flicked the pantry light on. There were several tiny black dots creeping over the surfaces of his food storage. They moved in tiny juts, crawling towards him. He closed his eyes, his stomach turned inside out. When he opened them again, the pantry was empty. A trick of the light. Or he was just that tired. His ear began to hurt again, eardrum throbbing. He flicked the light back off and decided he wasn't in a wine mood anyway.

He ate his lasagna in silence and went straight to

bed. It wasn't even nine o'clock when he fell asleep. He woke up at around three in the morning, desperately needing to pee. When he crawled back into bed, a tickling sensation swept across his face. He sleepily swatted at his nose, rubbing it. The wriggling moved up his forehead, across his cheek. His eyes jolted open. All he could see was the dark of the room, painted in muted shades of blue. He rubbed his eyes and turned onto his stomach. Sleep came crawling over him in shallow breaths.

He was staring at his front door. It stood enshrouded in a cloud of mist, as if it was the only thing that existed. The spider web curled in the corner, small like the first morning he saw it. His fingertips touched the silk and he pulled, tearing the thing apart in savage hungry motions. Here, he was God. He didn't notice the spider appear until it had crawled onto his hand in those jerking unnatural motions he had once read were unique to arachnids. They walked not with muscles but by pumping blood into and out of their legs at will. He froze, or rather, despite his brain's attempts, his body refused to move. The spider settled on his knuckle for a moment, then plunged its fangs into the delicate skin on the top of his hand. Pain seared through him. The spider wriggled, pushing through the holes it made until it was under his skin, tunneling through the bleary green veins. He could feel its hydraulic motion in his vessels, blood pumped in, pumped out, in, out. A juddering poison moving through the circulatory web of his arm up into his neck.

He awoke with his left arm throbbing, and his right ear aching in sympathy. It was morning, earlier than he needed to be up. The light in the room was a deeper grey than usual. He turned his phone alarm off and got out of bed. Coffee. He needed a coffee.

He sat in his kitchen, steam curling from the cup clenched in his hands. The window was open, in hopes that Athena might want to make an early visit, but so far, the only effect had been letting in the freezing air. The coffee was bitter against his tongue. It had been so long since he drank it first thing in the morning.

Time unwound around him. He checked his phone clock and realised his alarm had come and gone. He should have been getting out of the shower now. He ran his fingers through his hair. Greasy, but not too bad. It could go another day, maybe. When he brought his fingers down before his face to examine them, he jumped. A tiny black dot was hanging off his pinky, swaying from an invisible rope. He shook his hand furiously, the dot and the skin and the fingers blurring. When he stopped moving, the dot was gone. He examined the area around him, but it was nowhere.

A hunger pang passed through him. God, he thought, getting up to retrieve an orange from the fridge, his body worked like clockwork. When he turned back around, there was a spider the size of his fingernail on the table. His instincts kicked in. He brought the cold orange down on the creature with several days' vengeance. This had to be it. The front door web designer. The orange squelched under his palm, squirting juice onto his pajama shirt. He sighed. There. Over with.

When he lifted the orange, he could find no sign of

the spider. No disembodied legs, no black mark against the peel. There was no way he missed. It couldn't have escaped. He would have seen it. A thorough examination of the kitchen revealed nothing. No spider. Not even a dot. He took a deep breath and grabbed another orange out of the fridge. He needed to unwind. His stomach churned with coffee acid.

He pressed his thumbnail into the top of the orange and made the necessary first incision. As he peeled away the orange skin, it occurred to him how many white strands of nothing there were wrapped around the individual slices. He plucked one strand off with his index finger. It came away in a soft motion that drew goosebumps from his arms. He plucked another one off, and another. Soon he had a little pile of gossamer strands that he could barely look at without his ear starting to hurt. He rubbed the side of his head with his palm, wondering if he had an infection.

The stripped orange lay on the table before him, next to its nest of white strands. His gaze flicked from the fruit to the nest back to the fruit. A wash of nausea came over him. He stood up abruptly from the table, knocking his chair over. As he swept the deconstructed orange into the bin, he told himself he could just make an extra piece of toast at work again. The orange lurked at the bottom of the bin. He thought for a moment, then opened the fridge and discarded the rest of the orange pack as well. It thumped against the plastic like heavy rain. When it was over, and the bin was hidden away in its usual place again, he felt calm.

The calm didn't last through the workday. The web at his front door now overtook the entire top threshold, so he had to duck to get out. He spent most of the car ride with sore kidneys, morning coffee twitching at him. From the moment he sat at his desk, his concentration was shot. Every time he tilted his head back, the ends of his hair brushed the back of his neck and he found himself slapping at himself before remembering it was just his dire need for a haircut. Sometimes, he could see something brown moving in the corner of his eye. When he turned his gaze to face it, there was nothing there. His ear twinged. He opened a browser to look up earaches, which started by explaining that infections were the most common cause but eventually turned into a forum of people talking about bugs being pulled out of ears, which turned into videos of professionals removing centipedes from ear canals, which turned to his skin feeling like it was made of electrical current. He had to tear his gaze away from the computer screen and close out of the tab through squinted eyes. When that ordeal was over, he opened a new tab and looked up spider facts. The Goliath tarantula is big enough to hunt birds. Wolf spiders can occur at a density of three adults per square meter. Females lay up to eight thousand eggs. He left work early, muttering something about rhinovirus. No one questioned it.

On his drive home, his stomach grumbled. He had forgotten to make himself toast. The hunger, which had been kept at bay by shooting stabs of adrenaline, had now crashed back onto the shore. The shop was on the way home, and nearly empty at this time of day save the occasional retiree. He picked up a premade sandwich and remembered, as an afterthought, that he needed a new morning fruit. He turned towards the fruit and vegetable aisle, going the long way round to avoid the bin with the oranges.

Figs, it turned out, were on discount. It was a silly thought, but it occurred to him he had never tried a fig before. He bought two packs.

He had nothing to do when he got home. He wasn't used to being home in the day. It felt wrong, illicit, like he was breaking some rule he never knew existed. He flopped down on his sofa and turned on the TV. He'd eaten the sandwich in the car, so there wasn't even cooking he could distract himself with. A streaming service would have to do.

He watched a historical fiction series about some monarchs he somewhat remembered learning about in school. Spots flared before his eyes, sleepy clear circles bumping around the edges of his vision like a screen saver. One episode of monarchic drama slipped easily into the next. His eyelids drooped and he would have fallen asleep if it wasn't for the sudden movement he caught in the edge of his vision. A quick fluttering of legs in the upper corner of the living room. His eyes snapped to the offending image. Nothing. A bare wall. A shot of adrenaline. He readjusted and turned his attention back to the television. As his eyes zoned in on the screen, the edges of his vision wriggled, tiny black and brown flecks flitting towards him. Every one sent him jolting, desperately seeking out its source. But there was nothing. His ear began to ache, the tiny silver ball rolling around his ear canal. Tinnitus. He closed his eyes tight enough to see red flares. His head tilted back. Something brushed the back of his neck and he slapped at it, his palm finding the end of his hair. He needed a haircut. God. He wriggled around, trying to find a position on the couch where nothing touched his neck. Ghost pinpricks shivered up his spine. A wriggle of black crept into the edge of his vision.

The television played episode after episode before eventually pausing to ask him if he was still watching. He stared at the screen, frozen on the title sequence. By now, the sun had set, darkness pouring in through his open curtains. He blinked. It felt later than it was. It was that time of year. He hadn't realised how much the work day helped him regulate his sleep schedule. Without the commute home, the first signs of darkness made him want to curl up in bed.

He forced himself to have dinner first, moving through his nighttime routine like a puppet, disconnected from his body. His muscles ached. His ear hurt. His skin was an exposed nerve. A light breeze was enough to make him jump forward. As he brushed his teeth that night, it took every ounce of his will to stop himself from shaving his head right then and there. The strands of hair tortured him, dragging along the back of his neck.

That night, he didn't sleep. He only dreamt. He was in South Africa, on holiday with his university girlfriend. They had rented a beachside cottage for the weekend.

It was the Easter of their final year at uni. This was their last chance to do something like this. Back home, it was spring, the weather finally starting to turn over into pleasant, the sun a warm lamp, the sky a fragile blue. Here it was fall, the sky a blue so deep he felt himself gasping for air if he stared too long. How could the same sky be so different? The cottage was a small cozy thing with peeling orange paint. His girlfriend dropped her bag by the front door and began exploring their new terrain. He followed after. Giggling, holding hands. He tucked a strand of hair behind her ear and moved in to kiss her nose. A wriggle of brown caught his eye and he froze. She frowned, then followed his gaze. She froze too. It was the size of his hand, at least. Eight legs, eight eyes. Brown as dust. They stared at it. He bored his eyes into its fat torso as if his gaze could pin it in place. It didn't move. "Maybe it's dead," she offered. As if it had heard her, it took off, scampering towards anoth-er corner of the room. He shot back. They managed to track down a broom. The handle hit it with a wet crunch, maroon juice staining the floor like a Jackson Pollock. She opened her phone's internet browser. "Wolf spider. Not dangerous to humans," she said chirpily, as if that solved anything. He stared at the dark spot on the ground. They explored the house more cautiously after that. Every room they went in, there was another one. Anywhere you could expect a spider, there was a spider. Behind the bathroom curtain, under the coffee table, inside the kitchen drain. Each one they crunched down with the broom seemed to spawn three more somewhere else. When they got into bed that night, there were two waiting under their pillows. It was the first day of their holiday. As he lay awake in the darkness, he tried to count how many hours he had left in that house. A soft raking sound surrounded him, in the walls, in the ceiling, under the floorboards.

His eyes snapped open. The alarm on his phone had been going off for the last five minutes. He felt like melted candle wax. Sounds were muted. Time flicked by intermittently, like the carriages of a train. He couldn't quite fill in the gaps but one minute he was in the bathroom, the next standing before an open fridge, the next sitting at the table staring at a plate of figs, bloated purple-and-green sacs. The room was cold. Goosebumps crept up under his button-down. He had no idea how to eat a fig. He sniffed the skin, but it had no scent. He ran his fingernail along the edge of the fruit and it split into a sliver of red. He sniffed again. Vaguely floral. Using his thumbs, he pulled it apart at the seam, a sheath of stringy crimson dots dripping juice onto his plate. He frowned. It looked like something pulled out of an insect nest. Vaguely larval. His stomach growled. He took a bite. It was sweet and mealy, not in an unpleasant way. He grabbed another and opened his phone to scroll through a "How To" article about eating figs. The skin was fine to eat, apparently. At the bottom of the article, there was a fun fact section. He read through it, learning about the botanical origin of the fruit and which cuisines used it. He was nearly finished with the first fig when he came upon the final fact.

It sent him rocketing up towards the rubbish bin. He leaned over the plastic lip, retching. Wasps. He grabbed the remaining fruit in a frenzy. It disappeared quickly into the black chasm of the bin. He opened a new tab on his phone and read more, his stomach buzzing. Figs could be considered carnivorous. Wasps climbed into them to eat the fruit, but then couldn't get back out again. They died in the heart of the flesh, insect husks dissolved into nothing by the fig's enzymes. He stared at the figs at the bottom of the bin. Lumped together with the oranges, they looked like the blackened eggs of an abandoned nest. Shriveled stomachs. He shuddered, and before he could reflect more on what his own stomach was digesting, he saw it. Every muscle in his body tensed. There it was, in the corner of his eye. A writhing mass of black and brown creeping towards him. He kept his broom in the downstairs closet, several feet away. There was no time. His jaw locked. He'd had enough of the gossamer threat. This was fight or flight. He swiveled, heart pounding in his ears, and kicked. His foot connected with something solid and sent it flying. The feverish triumph burnt away quickly when he realised what he had done.

Athena lay on his tile floor yowling in pain. He stared, his brain flickering between thoughts like a faulty wire. He should call a doctor, or veterinary ambulance. He should call in sick. He should call a friend. He should check himself into a hospital. Something. All the strength drained from him, pooling out on the kitchen floor. He was tired. More tired than he had ever been.

The cat's shrieks followed him all the way to the bedroom, muffled only once he crawled into his bed. The lights were off, but the sun was finally starting to rise. All around him was an ashen grey. He closed his eyes. The throbbing in his ear hit a crescendo. He felt a popping sensation, then instant relief. Tiny dots spilled out of his ear, streaming down his face. It tickled, but he managed to keep his hands from smacking at the movement. There was nowhere to direct the slap. It was everywhere. It covered his skin so much he couldn't even feel his blanket. His ear rang, high and clear. When he opened his eyes, he could only see black, a mass of darkness writhing like so many tiny legs.

Fig. 6 — moths

EMPEROR

Saturnia pavonia (m.)

EMPEROR

Saturnia pavonia (f.)

OAK EGGAR

Lasiocampa quercus

BROAD-BORDERED YELLOW UNDERWING

Noctua fimbriata

LESSER YELLOW UNDERWING

Noctua comes

KENTISH GLORY

Endromis versicolora

PUSS

Cerura vinula

HERALD

Scoliopteryx libatrix

COPPER UNDERWING

Amphipyra pyramidea

ELEPHANT HAWK

Deilephila elpenor

DOUBLE LINE

Mythimna turca

MAGPIE

Abraxas grossulariata

EYED HAWK

Smerinthus ocellatus

THE BRONZE

Cacyreus marshalli

PRIVET HAWK

Sphinx ligustri

One Candle

Kathryn Leigh

I NGRID AND THE BABY LIVED ALONE IN A LARGE
house about two miles' walk from the edge of town.
They did not often have visitors, nor did they expect
to.

Ingrid had a moth collection of which she was very
proud. She kept them in a wooden display case, with
a glass front that she polished each morning. The old
house was full of moths, most of which she had already
catalogued. Occasionally, however, she would discover
a rarity among them. Catching moths was simple. Each
night after the sun had set Ingrid would extinguish every
candle in the house except for the one by her baby's crib.
She would wait until moths flew into the light, then
sweep in with a glass jar. If it was of no value she would
set it free, but if it was new she would keep it in her jar
until it died, and hope it didn't ruin its wings dashing
itself against the glass.

It was the beginning of autumn, and Ingrid was
working on her logbook, which contained technical
drawings of every moth in her collection. Her husband,

who was a naturalist and had been away for many years, kept walls and walls of such books in his study, which had been locked since his departure. Ingrid had never been able to find the key, and she imagined he had taken it with him on his journey. Either way, she had to work in the baby's nursery so she could keep a watch over it.

The moth she was drawing would not remain still, even though she had watched it die the previous day. It had been one of the tenacious ones, leaving dusty imprints all over the inside of the jar. Its broken antenna twitched. Ingrid sighed. It was a shame that it preferred to break itself, rather than suffocate with dignity. The moth's wing fluttered, still not resigned to its fate. Just a trick of the light. When the sketch was done Ingrid wrote its name, *Aglossa cuprina*, carefully on a small label. Then she took a pin from her pincushion and impaled the moth. As she did so, she thought she heard a sound from the baby's crib. She went over and looked down at its moon face.

"Why are you crying?" She asked. "Is your mother not here?"

She swept away a moth that had settled on its collar. She supposed they were drawn to its pale outfit. It had such a perfect mouth, like a painted doll.

"Your daddy will be home soon." Ingrid said, and she rocked the cradle in time with the grandfather clock ticking. It stood in the hallway but you could hear it all over the house. Ingrid was grateful for the clock's constant presence.

When it chimed seven, Ingrid made herself a small

dinner. Every Monday like clockwork a box of groceries
was delivered to the back doorstep, but Ingrid never
spoke to the delivery man. She didn't like to complain,
and supposed the arrangements were made by her
husband. This was the only delivery she ever received. As
she bathed herself and the baby after dinner she thought
about how in order to make silk, silk moth pupae were
boiled alive in their cocoons. The domesticated silk
moths that created the nightdress she was climbing into
were entirely reliant on humans for their reproduction,
unlike their wild cousins. Both types were beautiful,
white and strange. Ingrid would have been very excited
to see one, but she supposed she would never have the
opportunity to travel to the places where such things
live.

From her childhood, Ingrid understood that babies
were supposed to sleep all hours of the day, but when
she woke in the mornings and when she headed to bed
her child was always awake, watching her with its solemn
dark eyes. Each night she would read to it from Hooke's
Micrographia, which contained illustrations of plants
and insects under microscopes, and the observations
of the scientist Robert Hooke. Ingrid considered him a
great inspiration and was sure the baby was listening as
she relayed his discoveries. The pages of the book fluttered in the breeze as she read; Ingrid kept the upstairs
windows wide open all year, barring the dead of winter,
to beckon the moths inside. The flame of her candle
danced, but Ingrid was used to the dim light, and held
the book close to her face, so the baby could not see her

and she could not see it. When she was done reading she placed the book under the cradle and stood by the open window. Grime and cobwebs gathered at the corners of the panes, and beyond them the tangled lawn spread out like a square rag in front of the property. The trees seemed to stretch infinitely into the distance, though Ingrid knew there was a road a short walk beyond that would take her into town. The baby shuffled around, and she felt it looking at her back. The sky was clear and flat, and Ingrid knew the stars must be visible but she was short-sighted and had lost her spectacles. She must contact the eye doctor, she knew, but she couldn't head into town with her husband away and no one to care for her sickly baby. She saw the fuzzy outline of the moon, floating like a scrap of raw cotton.

Each day was much the same, as the nights drew in and grew cold. The trees around the garden turned vividly brown and shed their leaves onto the lawn. Ingrid's moth collection had grown stagnant, and she wanted to keep the windows open as long as possible to catch any unseasonal stragglers, so she stoked the fire and opened the chest where her winter cardigan was stored. Brown moths swarmed the chest; the cardigan was riddled with holes. Her husband's clothes, which she had stored here for safekeeping, fared no better. Betrayed, Ingrid boiled a bathful of water and threw the clothes into it. Once she was satisfied that all the clothes moths and their spawn were dead, she hung the clothes up in the garden. Her hands were red and dry, shocked from the boiling water and then the wintry air. Steam rose from the dripping clothes, suspended like condemned people. That evening, Ingrid was in a foul mood. The baby was crying and she ignored it, preferring to scrub the clothes chest and place lavender, rosemary, and peppercorns inside to deter the brown moths from ever returning. Eventually she returned to the nursery to stoke the fire. She picked her baby up and showed it the view of the garden. It seemed disinterested, and grizzled constantly.

"Why aren't you happy?" Ingrid asked.

As she tried to sleep that night, she kept thinking of the destroyed clothes. She imagined similar voracious larvae tearing through the books in her husband's locked study, consuming years of research while she struggled to open the door. She felt sick at the thought, and found herself awake until dawn, searching the house for the study key she had long given up hope of finding. Ingrid searched down the back of the breakfast room chairs not sat upon in years, and in among the still-hot ashes of the grate. When Ingrid searched behind the grandfather clock she found moth larvae writhing in the carpet, and crushed them under her foot. There was a distinction between the moths yet to be added to her collection, and these house invaders. Peering through the keyhole of the study, all Ingrid could see was dust.

She slept all of the following day between tending to the baby, but as the moon came up a thought occurred to her. It wouldn't be a great crime, she thought as she paced the nursery, to quickly go into town. She thought she remembered the doctor saying she should keep her baby inside until it was strong, but she could wrap it in blankets. It would be perfectly safe. She could visit the eye doctor, ask after a window cleaner, and she could fetch a locksmith, and perhaps even a midwife who could explain why herself and her baby were so patently unhappy. She could check the post office for a letter from her husband. Ingrid understood, as a woman of science herself, that trips like her husband's could be unpredictable and take people to far flung places, but he had been gone so long and was surely missing his family. She would close all the upstairs windows to make sure nothing crept inside. It would take two hours, at most. Ingrid felt better at this decision. She could open the study and see that nothing was amiss. She could even read to the baby from the books its father had written. Perhaps it would bring them both joy.

As Ingrid thought this, she saw movement in the garden below. She squinted and saw a human shape, but set it aside as just the movement of her clothes hanging on the line, until she felt the wool of her cardigan against her arms and realised that she had brought them inside days before, and that there was indeed a figure standing at the end of the garden in the shadow of the trees, staring up at her house. Ingrid held her candle up and light flashed back from the figure's eyes like a cat's. She thought for a moment the impossible, that her husband had heard their tears. But no, the figure walked without the pronounced limp, the slight stoop she remembered. It walked too quickly. Ingrid blinked and it was gone, and now stood beneath the black thread of the empty washing line, just outside the square of light cast by the window. It saw her candle before she had the chance to extinguish it or close the curtains, and now it was heading across the lawn towards the front door.

Ingrid backed away from the windows, kicking *Micrographia* under the cradle, in which the baby began to thrash and flail, crying tearlessly. There was a knock on the door downstairs. Ingrid stood in the nursery doorway. The grandfather clock chimed for one in the morning. In the dying fire, a log popped, and Ingrid heard a key turn in the lock downstairs.

"Delivery for Ingrid?" A voice carried up the stairs, and Ingrid frowned. At this hour? She smoothed down her nightdress and headed down, stopped just shy of the bottom step and watched the shadowed figure of the delivery man through the open door.

"Morning, madam." He said, stepping into the dim light. He wore a soft cap pulled low and a sheepskin jacket, and clutched a covered basket under one arm. "Your door was unlocked."

"Why are you out so late?" Ingrid asked, and he chuckled. She tried to remember if he was the same one who had brought their food before, but it was hard to recall.

"Terrible flooding on the road, madam." He said, and she saw that the hem of his jacket was gently dripping water. "Very dangerous. Practically impassable. Sure it'll sink back into the ground in a day or so."

Ingrid sighed, watching the basket as he placed it on the table. It was covered in a clean white linen, but the delivery man's hand was stained with soil. He pulled the linen back to reveal the contents. Maroon apples. Carrots fringed with green lace. Pears flushed pink. Cherries, roses, wide pale mushrooms, a cheese in wax paper, nasturtiums crowded together and beaded with floodwater.

"My husband goes to such great expense." Ingrid said, feeling her mouth beginning to water.

"I heard from the old folks that he's coming back soon." The delivery man said, smiling in a way Ingrid did not understand. "Perhaps even before winter ends."

Ingrid was silent, and the old house creaked around them. The man closed the front door, and the through breeze slammed a different door in the upper floor of the house. The screeching of the baby echoed down the stairs. Ingrid stared at the basket of produce, ravenous. The delivery man removed his hat, and his long, dark hair shook loose.

"Don't starve." He said, and Ingrid crossed the room to the basket. She took a pear and bit into it. The skin burst beneath her teeth. She had forgotten to eat until now. She crawled up onto the table. Her jaw worked faster than she could reach for more fruit. She spat out the grit from the unwashed carrots, and when she saw a worm hole in the apple she ate the bruised part first, then the seeds, then the core. The linen cloth was tough, and the wicker of the basket clawed the inside of her throat as it went down, but the taste was ambrosial. By the time she was sated, juice and mud dripping from her chin onto her nightdress, the delivery man was gone. She heard his footsteps above her, in the baby's room, where it lay screaming in its bed. She saw his handprint in the dust on the bannister as she ascended, and she avoided putting her hand in the same place. When she arrived in the nursery he was bent over the cradle.

"What are you doing?" Ingrid asked, as she always did. Her candle light deepened the shadows of his eye sockets. Mist sighed in through the open window.

"Are you looking after your precious baby?" He asked, putting his hands in for the baby to grab.

"Of course. He is more dear to me than anything in the world." Ingrid turned away from them to place her candle on the desk, where it seemed to animate her illustrations. There was a moth in the jar there that flew feebly towards the approaching light, hitting glass. When Ingrid turned back, the stranger was whispering to her baby, and for a moment in the moving shadows, Ingrid saw that he had moth wings under his clothes. When he undressed, the wings would spread and unfurl, grey, brown, and black.

The grandfather clock chimed, and had been chiming for a moment already.

"It's time for the baby to sleep." Ingrid said, feeling sweat on her forehead.

"Are you well, Ingrid?" The delivery man asked. "I hear there's a terrible fever around. Some folks in town died from it, I heard."

"Yes." Ingrid said, opening the nursery door. The handle stuck for a moment; she had to use all of her strength. The man hesitated in the doorway before her, and then he put his thin arms around and hugged her. He smelled like dead leaves, and she could feel her own heart beating ferociously. The breeze came in suddenly and blew out her candle, and as it did so she imagined taking the poker from the fire and impaling him with it, driving it into the wall next to her display case. He let go of her, and as she was fumbling on the desk for a match, she heard him leave the room. By the time she had lit the candle again, he was nowhere to be seen.

Ingrid was feeling really quite unwell, so she departed to bed barely having attended to the baby. When she tried her bedroom door it was locked, and she could not open it. She slept fitfully on the nursery floor. In the dead hours of the night she dreamed she heard her baby cry and stumbled to her feet, famished. As she bent over the crib she saw among the white sheets a cream-coloured grub the length of her forearm. It turned its sightless face towards her, its fat body concertinaing as she screamed, sobbed and held her candle against the sheets until it was burnt to death.

She woke up in a cold sweat, curled up on the ground, the wick of her candle almost entirely consumed. The dark hours of the morning still lingered, with no hint of dawn. The window was wide open above the still cradle, and the wind had scattered her illustrations across the floor around her. Ingrid pushed them aside, burdened with guilt, and stood up over the crib. She stared down at the sleeping baby, its perfect, placid doll's face. A moth had settled in the corner of its eye. Ingrid brushed it away. Her baby was the brightest thing in the room; it was no surprise they kept coming closer. More brown moths came and she swept them away, again, again and again.

Fig. 7 — dosette box

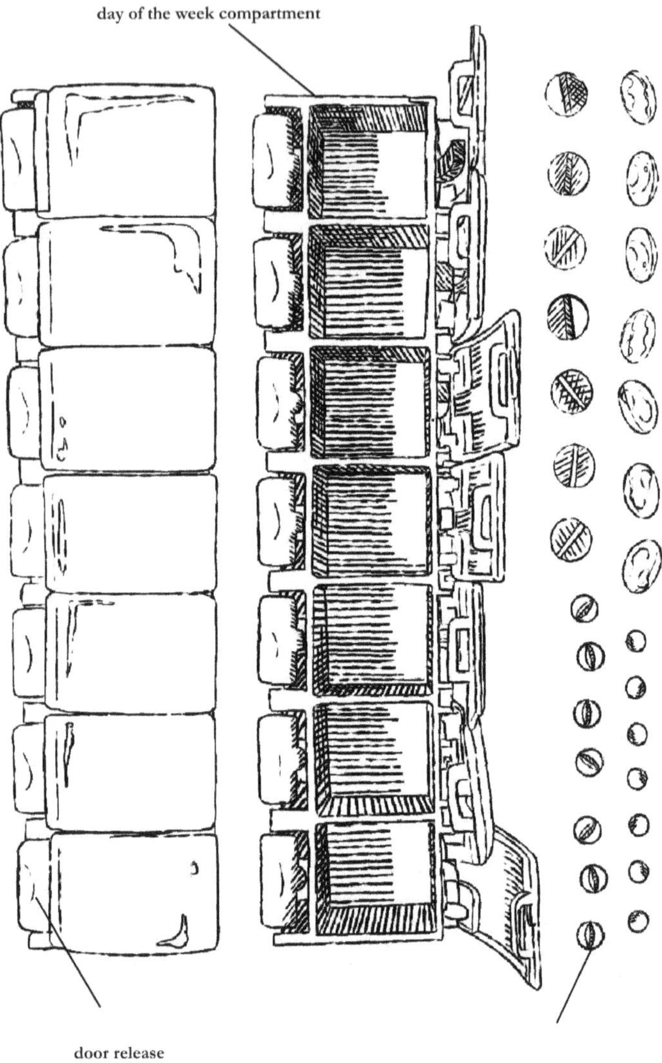

Dosette Box

Amber Donovan-Stevens

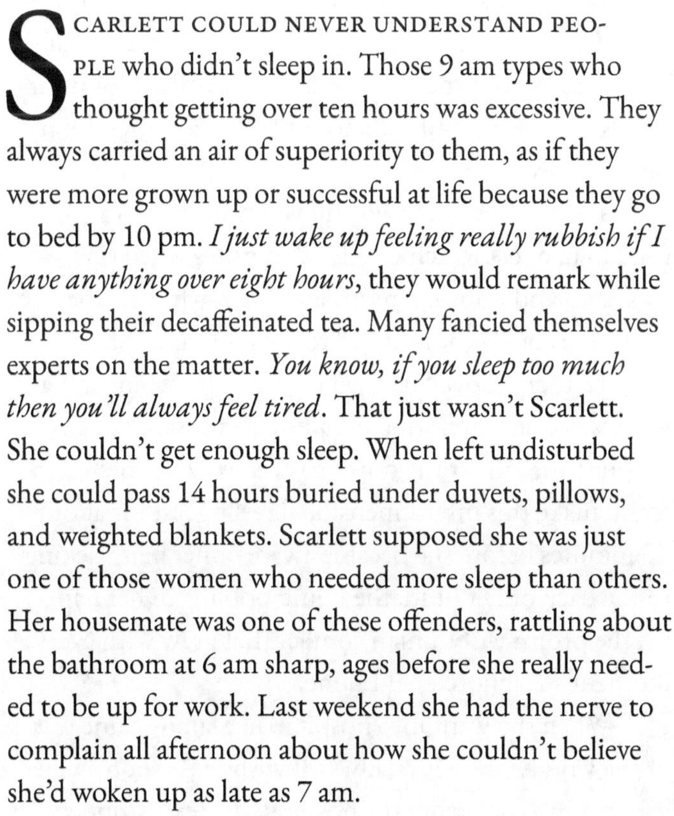

SCARLETT COULD NEVER UNDERSTAND PEO-
PLE who didn't sleep in. Those 9 am types who thought getting over ten hours was excessive. They always carried an air of superiority to them, as if they were more grown up or successful at life because they go to bed by 10 pm. *I just wake up feeling really rubbish if I have anything over eight hours*, they would remark while sipping their decaffeinated tea. Many fancied themselves experts on the matter. *You know, if you sleep too much then you'll always feel tired*. That just wasn't Scarlett. She couldn't get enough sleep. When left undisturbed she could pass 14 hours buried under duvets, pillows, and weighted blankets. Scarlett supposed she was just one of those women who needed more sleep than others. Her housemate was one of these offenders, rattling about the bathroom at 6 am sharp, ages before she really need-ed to be up for work. Last weekend she had the nerve to complain all afternoon about how she couldn't believe she'd woken up as late as 7 am.

In some ways, Scarlett believed she had hit the

jackpot with her sickness. She had a reason to never leave her bed and a selection of doctor's notes protected her from the daily text messages enquiring about her health from her work's HR team. She sat back in her dough-nut-shaped maternity pillow like she was in an inflatable dinghy. With just a little focus and imagination, her ochre-coloured duvet was a sandy beach, the wilted peace lily across the room a palm tree, and her nausea, reminiscent of a particularly choppy boat trip from Dover with her aunt in 2016, made her feel as if she was floating on open water. At sea, she would let her feet, hands, and elbows float and soften in the water until her cracked and bloody skin smoothed to wrinkles. She drifted for hours across the ocean until she succumbed to another dozen hours of sleep.

The world was always still when she came to. She used to nap just to achieve those minutes when one wakes up and nothing means anything, when the bed sheets are cool, and the mind feels as soft and full as a duck feather pillow. She tried to make the feeling last as long as possible, ignoring her phone and sticking one leg out from under the duvet to keep cool. At best, she could make this interdimensional feeling last for about 40 minutes before she became aware of her hair sticking to the back of her head, the liquid pooling in her nappy, the promise of human contact that grew with every moment she ignored her phone.

When she went into hospital, her family came out of the woodwork with daily well wishes. As soon as she was in a cab back from the hospital, the texts stopped.

The joints of her fingers and wrist ached as she held her phone over her face. WhatsApp. Nothing. Messenger. Nothing. Instagram. Nothing. E-mail. 25% off on best-selling vintage dresses this spring. Scarlett's hands cramped and she dropped her phone on the mattress, narrowly missing her face. She wondered how she would fit a nappy under her pencil skirts. The leaves on her peace lily had begun to brown at the tips. She thought of the crunch the leaves would make between her fingers.

The window in her room allowed a shard of orange light in during the golden hour, illuminating a wall of dust that appeared suspended in time. She wondered how many specks were floating in her room at that very moment. She wanted to protect her mouth and nose with her duvet, but she already wheezed without adding self-induced asphyxiation to the mix. Her breaths were shallow and drawn out. Sometimes Scarlett would suddenly gasp for air and she would realise she had gone a dozen seconds without breathing.

An alarm on her phone went off and she stiffened. She glanced at the towers of various unopened boxes of medications on her bedside dressers and wondered how long it would take her to pry open a single box. She craned her arm to retrieve her phone. *20:00 - Pls take meds.* She sighed and tapped the snooze button and dropped the phone back on the mattress.

A dreamcatcher hung from the curtain pole at the window. It had a big clear bead in the centre that caught the light during sunset, refracted a glimmer onto a small pink conch made of glass, which she'd gotten from a boot fair when she was a child. The conch sat on her bookshelf and, in the golden hour, looked more like a lump of flesh dipped in a glittery oil than tempered glass. Around this time each evening she would watch it shimmer. It was the highlight of her day, if she was awake to see it.

Swathes of feathery cobwebs hung from the dream-catcher but she had yet to see the spider who had left the silken mess. Many a party of creepy crawlies had passed through their mid-terrace let. The daddy long-legs joined them for the first semester of each academic year and always left early for Christmas. The slug situation only intensified as it seemed that for every slug she put outside, two more found their way into the downstairs bathroom. And the woodlice stopped by, just once, to celebrate her graduation. Of course, there were also the "misc. spiders" who had their own routine. The thick ones that would hurtle across her living room floor on movie night and send her housemates into a shrieking frenzy as they jumped from sofa to armchair. She had found that a ramekin and a cardboard envelope were the ultimate tools in helping them on their way. Sturdy yet smooth. She wanted the bug to feel swept into the ramekin, not tripped in, she explained to her housemates, who applauded her precision and bravery. So, whenever guests with wings or more than two legs announced themselves, her housemates fled to their room and left the resident entomologist to "take care of them." Scarlett chased daddy long-legs out of the back door, wafted wasps back out the window, and deployed a teaspoon of table salt on any slug that would apparate into the downstairs bathroom. She drew the line at snails though. She couldn't bring herself to rain salty hell on a gastropod with its home on its back.

The phone alarm shrilled again. *20:05 - Pls take meds.*

To the right of her bed, amongst the towers of medication on the dresser, was a fresh glass of water and an espresso cup containing a thimble of yellow viscous liquid. With sloth-like agility, she arched from her maternity pillow to reach the cup. She felt the stretch of a back muscle that spread down her spine and connected with pain from deep inside. She fell back into the pillow, holding the espresso cup upright in the air. She tipped the sweet liquid into her mouth, holding the cup back as the 10 mL of Oramorph oozed its way down her oesophagus. She stuck her tongue into the cup and wiped it around the inside, savouring any residue of the sap. Holding the cool porcelain to her crusted lips, she closed her eyes and sighed.

The woodlice—or rollie pollies as her American housemate identified them—were a funny thing. The visitation happened on the night of her graduation. Scarlett had put a wet scrunchie on the mantlepiece of the boarded fireplace in her room. She went out for drinks after the ceremony and came back to find a small battalion of woodlice congregating around the scrunchie. She watched them for a while, their little antennae moving about as if in discussion with one another. There had been no woodlice sightings prior to this and now here they were, just hanging out. Scarlett hadn't paid much attention to woodlice since she had been at primary school. She greeted each one as "Gary" and, several ciders gone, had asked them what they were nattering about, and if any of them fancied a spot of damp wood from the garden. In the end, she left them to it and passed out on her bed. She woke up to a deserted mantlepiece, dry scrunchie, and splitting headache.

She recalled the first time she met the little shelled creatures. *Woodlice are the nits of wood*, her teacher Mrs Minsie had declared on a trip to the potting shed in year one with her class. Scarlett remembered it well as Mrs Minsie had directed this at a girl in her class—Jenny C— with perpetual nits. Mrs Minsie gathered them around an old wood stump and lifted it onto its side, revealing dozens and dozens and dozens of creepy crawlies and a couple of fat slugs. The other children stamped across the dirt to see the society under the stump.

"Rollie pollies!" Shouted Jack L.

Scarlett remained on the path to the potting shed in her yellow wellies.

"Yes Jack! Very good. These are woodlice."

Scarlett peered around the children. The rotting wood had long grooves that looked like hair. She watched the woodlice flee, the centipedes march out, and the fat slugs stay put. She took a step closer, careful to avoid any of the bugs that had been woken and chased onto the path.

"Look Scarlett!"

She turned to see Tommy B grinning as he held

a woodlouse up between his finger and thumb. She watched its hairline antennae feel about Tommy's thumb, and 14 legs try to crawl free.

"Look I can make him poo!"

He squeezed the woodlice between his finger and thumb until a murky puss squeezed from its end. Scarlett froze. Slowly, its feelers and legs stopped moving. Tommy B boomed with laughter, turning from her to find another woodlouse and classmate to perform his joke to. She looked back to the circular indent in the mud left by the stump. There were only a couple of woodlice remaining. She crouched at the edge of the path to watch them. One crawled onto the stone. She took a deep breath and placed her finger on the slab. The woodlice clambered aboard, and she very slowly stood up. She watched the woodlouse use his many fibrous legs to travel along her finger. She decided to name him Gary, as he looked like one. She alternated fingers to create an ongoing path for him, his dark grey shell shiny in the light. If only she could—she touched his shell and Gary rolled into a ball off of her finger. She gasped and caught him with her open palm. He remained in a ball. Wide eyed, she glared at him. Had he died? She tried to keep her hand still. Slowly, his feelers emerged, as if checking for trouble. Gradually, he returned to his normal shape and resumed his journey across her palm. She guided him onto her finger and placed him on the underside of the overturned stump. She whispered a goodbye to Gary and rejoined her classmates who were seeing who could grab the most worms. Since then, every woodlouse was called Gary.

There was a twang from within the wall and the walls gurgled to heat the radiators. She ran her tongue across the cracks on her bottom lip, which tasted metallic. Cotton mouth made her saliva stringy and she felt her oesophagus was drying out inch by inch. Deep down beyond her oesophagus, there was burning, as if something had reached into her and clamped her stomach once, hard, and it had yet to regain its bean shape. She sunk back into the pillow, leaving the espresso cup next to her on the mattress.

Scarlett dreams she is back in hospital. The incessant beeping from across the ward reminds her that she is a guest, and the starched sheets of the hospital bed draw blood from her elbows. Doctors stand over her, their faces obstructed by a blinding orange light. She scrunches her eyes shut and holds her breath to avoid drying her nostrils and lips out any further. She retracts within herself, layer by layer. Somewhere below the sheets of dried skin are sopping intestines, infected with an occasional charge that causes them to spasm. She wants to turn herself inside out, so the dry might finally be wet. She starts with her bottom lip and peels it back over her chin. The beeping grows louder. Her nails catch open like the hood of a car, and she starts to pull her red fingertips through. But the next charge in her intestines is so painful that she is sure her insides are being squeezed out of her. The beeping is deafening. She flings her eyes open to the doctor who must be torturing her and sees only white.

Scarlett woke up to a beeping that came from the

washing machine in the kitchen and a heavy weight on her abdomen. Her bedroom light was on and the towers of medication on the vanity by her bed had been pushed back out of arm's reach to make room for a plate of toast, evenly covered to the edges with butter and jam, as well as a cold glass of water. There was no new espresso cup. Instead, on the plate next to the piece of toast was a pill box no bigger than a chocolate bar. She steadied her breath and grasped for the pill box. She held it above her face. Each lid was a colour of the rainbow and had the days of the week abbreviated and printed on them. A drop of butter had dripped off the toast and greased SUN. They had another name. What was it? Dosser box? No, of course not. It was more French than that. Dosette box!

As far as Scarlett was concerned, only wrinkly people used a dosette box. She first saw a dosette box when she was a toddler, nosing about her nana's bathroom one summer. The avocado suite had check cream walls that were cigarette-stained yellow and a medicine cabinet with mirrored doors held shut by a single brass hook that Scarlett could open if she stood on the wicker footstool. Like the one she now had, the seven-doored box was a little bigger than her palm, with the abbreviated days of the week printed on each lid. Inside were non-descript pink and yellow pills, much too big for swallowing. Scarlett shook it like a maraca. Silly Nana should've used it as a chocolate calendar, or put Skittles in it, though Nana didn't like sweets. If she ever asked for sweeties, Nana would tell her that if she really wanted something sweet,

she could have a teaspoon of honey. At supper, she asked
Nana if she could have her own little box, to which all
the adults laughed. Dosette boxes popped up from time
to time over the years, hanging from a revolving display
in pharmacies, sun-faded amongst old crockery at boot
fairs, and on the bedside table of people who were long
gone by the time she finished secondary school. As Scarlett left for university, surrounding herself with young
people, in a county that only hosted boot fairs outside of
the city, she'd all but forgotten about them.

Scarlett turned the dosette box in her hand. There
would be absolutely no fitting the two dozen pills she
needed to take each day into the square centimetre boxes.
She opened and closed MON. She reached and placed
it back on the plate. She ran two fingers across her toast,
scooping up as much jam as possible. Her housemate
had busted out the Lurpak. She stuck her jammy fingers
in her mouth and ran her fingers across her tongue. She
closed her eyes, let out a long sigh, and sunk back into
her bed a little. She paused and opened her eyes. Removing her fingers from her mouth, she inspected them, then
inspected the plate of toast. For so long her mouth had
simply tasted dry but now she could have sworn that,
after the sweet rush of raspberry jam, she could taste
what could only be described as the fermented, muddy
taste of faeces.

A lump stuck in the back of her throat. She began
to weep but no tears emerged. Outside, kids shrieked
to one another and the sound of buggy wheels rolling
against the pavement passed by the window from the

afternoon school run.

Scarlett woke up to her alarm and a pain that coursed through her stomach. *20:00 - Pls take meds.* She let out a moan and reached under her maternity pillow to retrieve her phone. It was 21:03. The lights were out and the curtains were still open, letting in the street light. Almost every night she thought of how much she had taken closing her curtains for granted. In the dim light she couldn't identify the shadowy towers of medication. Nor could she see a new espresso cup. The streetlight illuminated the dust and debris that had gathered on her water. Her right side felt numb but it would take her at least 20 minutes to turn over onto her other side. She continued to lay on her side. Baby steps. She tried to focus on the rise and fall of her body as she breathed. A single deep breath and she rolled from her side onto her back. White hot pain shot through her colon. Steady-ing her breathing, she stared at the artex on the ceiling. When she was a little girl in nappies her father had lifted her onto his shoulders and laughed that she smelled pongy. Sitting on his shoulders, she was so high up that she could touch the ceiling of her childhood kitchen. She thought of how the paint that had dried all swirly and stippled had felt sharp against her fingertips. Now, in the ground floor bedroom of her university digs, the ceiling felt so low that she might reach it from bed. She reached her arm up to the ceiling to touch it. The ceiling was definitely lower than before. Her arm gave out and dropped down beside her; she stared at the ceiling light until her vision blurred.

When Scarlett comes to, she hears the hoot of an owl outside and the moon illuminates her dresser. Her lips rasp across one another and she tongues the ulcers that have developed across her gums. The shooting pains in her intestines are irregular and sharp. Her nappy irritates her skin and her hips are raw from where the plastic chafes. She turns her shoulders to grab a new espresso cup of Oramorph on her dresser but fingers don't touch porcelain. In the dark, she can just about make out her dosette box and a glass of water, nothing else. Feeling betrayed, the ache in her stomach gives way to a rage that bubbles within her. She can't believe that her housemates have denied her a thimble of Oramorph. In the absence of the espresso cup, she hopes that they might have at least given her some paracetamol, so she reaches for the box, careful not to disturb deep pain further. Partially laying on her side, she looks across the doors and picks one at random. Her hands fumble with the WED door. Soon she pops the door open to find a grey shelled ball, smaller than a pea, inside the box. She recoils and slams the door shut. The sudden jolt sends hairline pains to her stomach and she grips the pill box until her knuckles are white. How in God's name did he get in there? The box shakes in her hand and as her breathing evens out she softens her grip and examines the box. She opens WED again and sees the woodlouse still in his ball. This time she closes the door gently. She moves to open THUR, her fingers slowed, arthritic-like pain dulled by the adrenaline rush. She shrieks as she sees two curled up woodlice roll inside THUR. This is too sick a joke for her housemates. She opens MON, TUE, FRI, SAT, and SUN to reveal a dozen woodlice rolled up in balls. The box shudders in her hands and all the Garys roll about in their boxes. She pops WED back open and places the dosette box back on her dresser. Displaced from her usual position, she lies face down on her maternity pillow, smelling grease and tasting acid in the back of her throat. She shrieks into her pillow.

Scarlett's lips touched something wet. She realised she had soaked some of her pillow with dribble. She remained still, listening for her housemates thudding around upstairs or the occasional thwack the neighbour's tree made on her window. It was black outside and she could see her own room reflected back at her on the window glass. She can't see herself in the reflection. Her bed looked messy as if no one was asleep in it. She listened to the muffled sound of wind crashing up and down the street. Chattering passed by her bedroom window. The iron gate to the house crashed against the brick wall. She flinched and the pain in her body sparked back up. The voices bustled out with the wind. She wished for a moment that her bed was out on the street and that she could feel the air beat against her face or the rain spit on her peeling skin. Outside, she could hear the sound of her housemates fighting against the wind with their drunken exchanges, proud in the black. As she looked to her window she caught sight of the bottle of Oramorph on the shelf below her conch. Had it been there all this time? Exalted, she returned her head to the pillow, placing her lips back to the spot where she dribbled and listened to the whistle of the boarded fireplace. Tomorrow, she will have that bottle.

The sound of pots and pans clanging from the kitchen clash against the muffled sound of Heart FM. A voice crooned along with Phil Collins and another voice heckled the flat rendition of "In The Air Tonight." Scarlett's room is bright and her bedsheets feel cool. She looks at the bottle on her shelf. Still there. She looks to the dresser and sees a ramekin brimming with Skittles. She gasps, grabs at the ramekin and flinches at her own sudden movement. Ramekin in hand, she grapples with her pillow and props herself up a little. She grins and licks her lips.

"Thaaaaank you!" she shouts at the house. The clattering and singing continues.

She pops one in her mouth and glides it along her tongue until the sugary shell softens. The sweet raspberry flavour that fills her mouth makes her salivate. She pops another in her mouth and savours it less this time. She rushes to eat every colour of the rainbow. She begins eating two or three at a time, crushing them without tasting them or stopping for breath. She gasps as she gulps them down. They crush between her molars with less crunch and as she pops sweet after sweet, the fruity flavour gives way to a bitter and metallic taste. The shells stick in her mouth, smooth against her tongue, but the inside of the sweet transforms from chewy sweet to a zany goo that claws at the back of her throat. Her brain only registers this as the bitter goo is halfway to her stomach. She retches and gags her mouthful onto her duvet. The pain caused by her sudden movements causes her to spew further. In amongst the swirl of candy-coloured saliva are the remnants of chewed woodlice, their legs scattered like grains of rice. She recoils and the sudden movements fill her with pain. She continues to gag, writhing into a ball until there is nothing left. Hoarse, her heaves give way to sobs and she begins crying until she wails and wails until she's screaming. Head pounding, crusty lips stained cherry, and eyes puffed shut, she can't hear the clattering of pots and pans. She can't hear the hum of Heart FM.

The neighbour's car alarm woke her. Her cheeks were burning and her legs stuck together. She shunted her duvet off of herself. The smell of her nappie curdled her taste buds. Despite the pain pulsating around her intestines, her legs and head were numb. She ran her hand across the mattress for her phone. 19:04. She could no longer hold her phone with one hand. She had a missed text from the HR manager: *Hi Scarlett. Hope you're feeling better. Are you coming into the office on Monday? Just a reminder that if you won't attending the office then we will require a signed doctor's note from—*

Her fingers cramped and she dropped her phone square on her nose. She felt heat rush to the centre of her face. She curled to the right, clutching her nose until it stopped pulsating. There was no new espresso cup on her dresser.

"Guys?"

She's out of volume. Her second call was even weaker.

Her bedroom has most certainly shrunk. If she could reach her arm up she would surely be able to touch the ceiling. She looks at the bottle on the shelf. It's closer than before. The wall twanged as the heating came on.

She has to get back to the sea. When Scarlett is at sea, there is no need for nappies, Vaseline, or maternity pillows. She would rest her dried skin in the water, and she would bleed into the salt.

She takes a deep breath and rotates to the right: first her hips, then her shoulders. Rolling over the doughnut-shaped maternity pillow causes a scream to rip out of her throat from her abdomen. She feels liquid swash in her nappy and she huddles in a ball on the edge of her bed until the pain simmers down. She looks at the Oramorph bottle across the room. The shelf is about six feet away.

Still lying on her side, she lowers one leg off the bed. She heaves and grips her pillows to herself for support or comfort, she can't tell. The other leg she edges a centimetre at a time, each movement causing a flare of pain in her knees and between her legs. She wobbles the vanity by her bed for support as she tries to lower herself, but her wrist cramps, and she thumps to her knees, and falls on her side. Her knees burn and the pushing in her pelvis grows.

She shivers against the touch of the floor. She takes a moment to steady her breathing. From down here, she sees dust under her vanity, a pink scrunchie wreathed in cobwebs, and a yellowing piece of paper folded on itself and tucked under a leg of the vanity to balance it. She places both her palms against the floorboards and lightly pushes against the floor. Her wrists collapse and she thumps down stomach-first, sending dust into the air.

She wiggles against the floor, and for a while, she is not making any distance from the bed. She draws her knees in to push herself forward, but this sends a lightning bolt of pain through the organs in her middle. She reaches her arms out and slowly props herself up by her forearms. She pants as she pulls herself across the floorboards on her forearms, balling her fists in determination, her joints flaring with fire. She enters the orange light cast from the window as she reaches the foot of the bookshelf.

She pants, catches her breath, and relaxes her body against the floor. She looks up at the bottle on the fourth shelf. It is at least two arms away from her. The lump in her throat escapes and she lets out a whimper. She weeps against her forearm. The pushing from her pelvis is bigger than the world. Something is going to push its way out of her and she doesn't know what will be left of her when it does. She takes deep breaths and looks up at the bottle. She grips the first level of the shelf, digging in her fingers, nails snapped back and bloodied, and uses her whole body to shake the shelf toward her. She wails, rattling the shelf and the bottle falls from the sky, bouncing off the floor and rolling in a circle. The spine of her complete *Principles of Insect Morphology* collection also comes off the shelf and hits her on the brow. The conch follows, smashing inches from her head, sending fragments ricocheting into her skin. She curls her body into the shelf as defence until she is certain the hail stopped. A laugh emerges from among her wheezes.

She unhooks her fingers from the shelf and claws her way to the bottle, letting out a growl at the end of each breath. She seizes the bottle, fingers cramping as she wrangles with the child-proof cap of the Oramorph. The cap comes free and she spills a glob onto her wrist. She lets out a yelp in exaltation and laps the liquid from her wrist. She clutches the lid in her withered fingers, wraps her lips around the bottle, and takes one glug, two glug, three glug. She rubs her chapped lips on the bottle. The sweet thick liquid coats her bloodied lips. She lets the third glug sit on her tongue, sweet and thick. It smooths over the walls of her throat as if to galvanise her. This thin, sweet coating holds back the host of pains. Finally, her mouth isn't dry.

Her breathing softens. She loosely screws the cap on and holds the bottle to her stomach as she retracts into the foetal position. The flames that raged in her joints die to faint licks. The pulsing heat in her face fades. The pushing in her pelvis retreats. The dust around her head floats in its place and the shards of broken glass sparkle in the golden hour. She presses her cheek against the wooden slat of the floor and dust and hair comes away on her cheek.

She watches the boarded fireplace and listens to the whistle of the chimney. A woodlouse emerges from a crack in the wood. She closes her eyes and counts in her head how long she can go without breathing. Her cheek presses to the sandy slats of a beach dock in June. The sea twinkles against the sunset. In a while, her Nana will find her and offer her a teaspoon of honey.

Fig. 8 — cassette tape

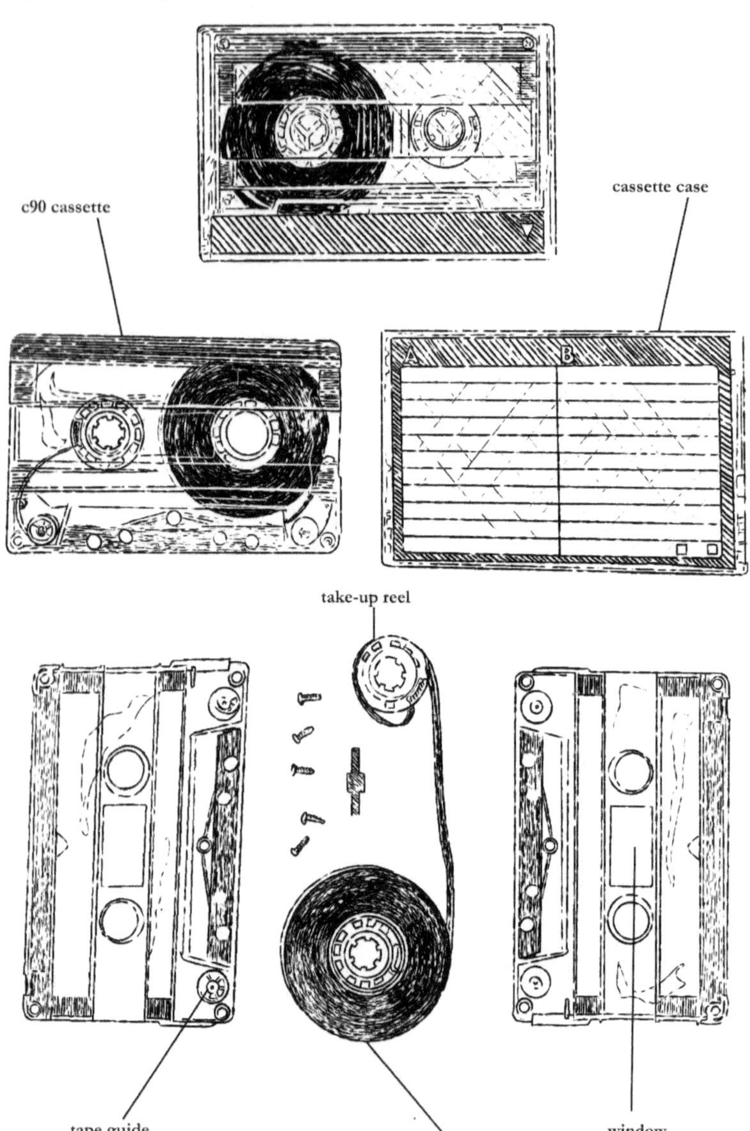

Tapes

Kathryn Leigh

I'M IN THE SPARE BEDROOM AT MY PARENTS' house when I get the call. A young American woman. She says she's heard of my work, and wants to know whether I might like to write a memoir of her grandmother. I flick some crumbs off my duvet and tell her I'm not a memoirist. She tells me that her grandmother was Mary Olden, and I tell her I'll be on the next plane.

Mary Olden is my hero. The best poet in the twentieth century, when I'm being conservative; the best poet who ever lived if I've had more than two beers. I've devoted my whole career to her, a thankless calling that has left me living in my parent's spare room, inhaling my own sweat, newly single, and clinging to my mobile phone in a daze. Mary Olden's granddaughter tells me that she's been bequeathed a box of old tapes, the last recordings of her grandmother alive. A long fuss over the will, she says, embarrassing family squabbling. But she has them now, and would I like to come and transcribe them? My heart races so hard I can hear the pulse in my wrist.

Mary Olden lived in a house in the deep South, but I land in New York City to meet her granddaughter. On the plane I imagine the long drive to the Olden family home, stepping out of the car to inhale sludgy, green-tasting air, the irrepressible heat, looking up at the white wooden facade behind which Mary Olden once paced, brewing up poetry to electrify me.

The younger Ms Olden is skinny and tired-looking in the white light of the airport. The overnight flight has me discombobulated.

We finally sold the creaky old Louisiana place, she says in the taxi. Who wants to live in a plantation house? Doesn't seem right.

Oh, I say. That makes sense.

Nothing but wormwood, snakes, and ghosts, she continues. Good riddance.

Quite right, I say. My chest aches, and I blame travel anxiety.

Her small apartment on the 10th floor is cold. There's mould in the bathroom. The paint's peeling. It's like everywhere I've ever lived. A lone 25th birthday card with specks of sauce splattered on it is attached to the refrigerator.

Ms Olden waits long enough to boil me a cup of water in the microwave before she asks, So, you think people will buy the memoir?

Yes, I do, I say. I drop a dusty green tea bag into my boiling cup. The handle is too hot.

The money would be nice. She looks embarrassed.

Yes. It would.

We make an agreement to split the royalties fifty/ fifty. I feel like I'm trampling gently on Mary Olden's grave. I'm excited to be so close to her.

Hearing Mary Olden speak is strange and wonderful. She was a famous recluse, and never once gave an interview; probably a blessing given how exposure taints true art. I imagined her voice as commanding, resonant, charismatic; a voice that could bear the weight of her poetry. Instead, it is soft, slow, a drawl, like a long day.

Somebody had better listen to these, she says on one recording.

These are my last rites, she says on another. I noted that down as a potential title for the book.

I just want to see her before I die. She says on a third. I have "her" outlined, underlined, highlighted, and circled. I have a family tree drawn up. Mary Olden's literary circles are vague and undocumented despite my best efforts. Who is *she*? Ms Olden says she doesn't know. A girlfriend? Her grandmother had friends and lovers, ex-lovers, enemies. She smoked cigars with ever-changing groups of them while a five-year-old Ms Olden stood in the corner, fascinated. One had scarlet lips, one had a blue hat, one leaned heavy on a cane, one had jowls that hung loose like a bulldog's. All came and went namelessly in the fog of Ms Olden's childhood memories.

She never mentioned anyone she wanted to see, Ms

Olden said, and by the end she wouldn't have anyone to visit anyway.

There are 112 tapes, some mostly blank save a couple of minutes, others half an hour long. I spend the first eight days holed up in Ms Olden's apartment, in amongst a tangle of wires, with headphones plugged in my ears. Mary just has—had—so much to say. I don't hear half as much from Ms Olden the younger. She works in a restaurant, and when she does come over to check on our progress, she tends to smoke and look nervous.

Why was it so hard for you to get hold of these tapes? I say on the ninth day, while Ms Olden shows me some photographs of her grandmother. Mary wears black dresses, lace gloves, and always looks away from the camera. She is hunched like a vulture, even in her younger days.

Ms Olden sighs, leaning back on the faded couch. Empty takeaway containers are stacked on the floor between us.

Well, originally, they were bequeathed to my mother in the will. So that was trouble.

Why trouble?

My mother went missing five years ago.

Went missing? I'm so sorry. Did she...

Who knows? I was in college. Maybe she was waiting for me to leave.

I look up from the pictures of Mary Olden and watch her granddaughter instead. My host's face is prematurely lined with grief. There is faint family resemblance, like a greasy fingerprint.

When we sold the Louisiana place we figured Mother wasn't coming back for the tapes, so we took them, she continues. Well, she's missing out, I say, and then am embarrassed as I realise that, for once, I am not talking about the tapes.

Ms Olden laughs, not looking at me. When she laughs, the family resemblance is almost gone.

Ms Olden's name is Ruby.

I have a favourite tape. In it, Mary Olden sounds strong, intent.

Poetry must be passed down, from mother, to daughter, to granddaughter, and so on. It can't live otherwise. It needs blood, like a creeper needs water. The roots will push until they find it, too.

I can imagine the four-poster bed in which the old woman sits, the Louisiana heat creeping through the window. In the background of the recording, the door creaks. I go to press STOP, and hear footsteps. I jump, swivel in my chair. The apartment is empty. It's well after two in the morning; Ruby is asleep.

The footsteps are recorded.

I stop the tape, and pop open the tape player. There on the label: mother, daughter, granddaughter.

I have listened to these tapes dozens of times, meticulously numbered and titled them. And I know that this one ends just as the door creaks. I double-check my transcript. No footsteps.

Fascinated, I put the tape back in and adjust my headphones.

The footsteps continue and stop.

Well, well. I didn't think you'd come.

A new woman's voice. Not Mary's. *I'm here now, aren't I?*

Oh, I'm so glad. I just wanted to see you before I die.

The tape crackles and stops. I don't wake Ruby.

I tell her the next morning, when she's done eating her cereal. My hands shake as I hand her the headphones.

Ruby listens. She goes pale.

That's my mother's voice.

Your mother!

She never told me she went to visit grandmother. I thought they hated each other.

Ruby rewinds the tape, unplugs the headphones. We both listen.

The tape crackles.

Footsteps.

I didn't think you'd—

Wait, I say, rewind to the start.

This is the start, Ruby says.

I look at the tape, and she is right.

But half of it is missing.

Maybe there was a kink in the reel, or something.

A door slams in the apartment above. The tape

crackles.

I didn't think you'd come.

Well, I'm here now, aren't I?

Oh, I'm so glad. I just wanted to see you before I die. Ruby's mother continues.

I just want to see her before I die.

Oh, me too. I just want to see her before I die.

I just want to see her before I die.

The tape clicks and ends. I flip to a fresh page in my notebook, scribbling down the new transcription. Ruby listens again. And again. I go to the bathroom. Ruby listens.

I just want to see Mary before I die. The tape says.

Mary?

Ruby removes the headphones slowly; a strand of her hair tangles around the cord. I need to go, I've got work.

Who's Mary? I ask, but she's grabbing her things. Are you alright?

I'm fine. Just don't want to be late, she says, leaving in a rush.

I see her from the window of the apartment, walking in a green coat. She disappears into the crowd.

I am intent on understanding. I listen to the tapes again, but they've changed. 32: "Treatise on Gentlemen," 47: "The Roof Is Leaking," 87: "I Hear Cicadas In My Dreams" all now say the same thing. Two voices.

I just want to see Mary before I die.

I listen to 112: "Mother, Daughter, Granddaughter" so many times I begin to hear footsteps where there are none. When it gets to midnight and Ruby isn't home, I walk three blocks to the restaurant where she works. It's closed up for the night, dark inside. When I get back to the apartment, the tape I left in the tape player is all unspooled on the floor like a long, black ribbon. I take a pen and wind it back up.

I just want to see Mary before I die.

I call Ruby six times, and I realise I don't know anyone she knows. I go to the restaurant in the daytime, and when I ask for Ruby the people there just shrug.

After a week of waiting I call my parents and tell them I'm coming home. Ruby's phone won't take calls anymore. I'm too worried about her to care about the loss of Mary's recordings, cannibalising themselves somehow within the reel.

On the twenty-fifth day, someone bangs on the door. I stay crouched by the sofa where I'm packing up the tapes, too scared to open it. I hear something paper slide under the gap that always kept the room so draughty.

Later, I gather my courage, and go to collect the envelope that's been slipped under the door. It's marked IMPORTANT in bold letters. Overdue rent? I see this address. My hands shake. I see the addressee.

Mary Olden. Mary Olden. Mary Ruby Olden.

———⟨◇⟩———

Should I call the police? What if they think it was me?

I listen to 112 again.

The door creaks. Footsteps.

I didn't think you'd come.

Well, I'm here now, aren't I?

Not Ruby's mother's voice anymore. Ruby's voice.

Oh, I'm so glad. I just wanted to see you before I die.
The older women chorus.

I can't move.

There's just one thing. Ruby says. The tape has already run to its end.

There are footsteps. The door creaks. A warm Louisiana breeze.

I hear her voice beside my ear.

I just want to see you before I die, Mary says.

I just want to see you before I die.

Fig. 9 — eggs

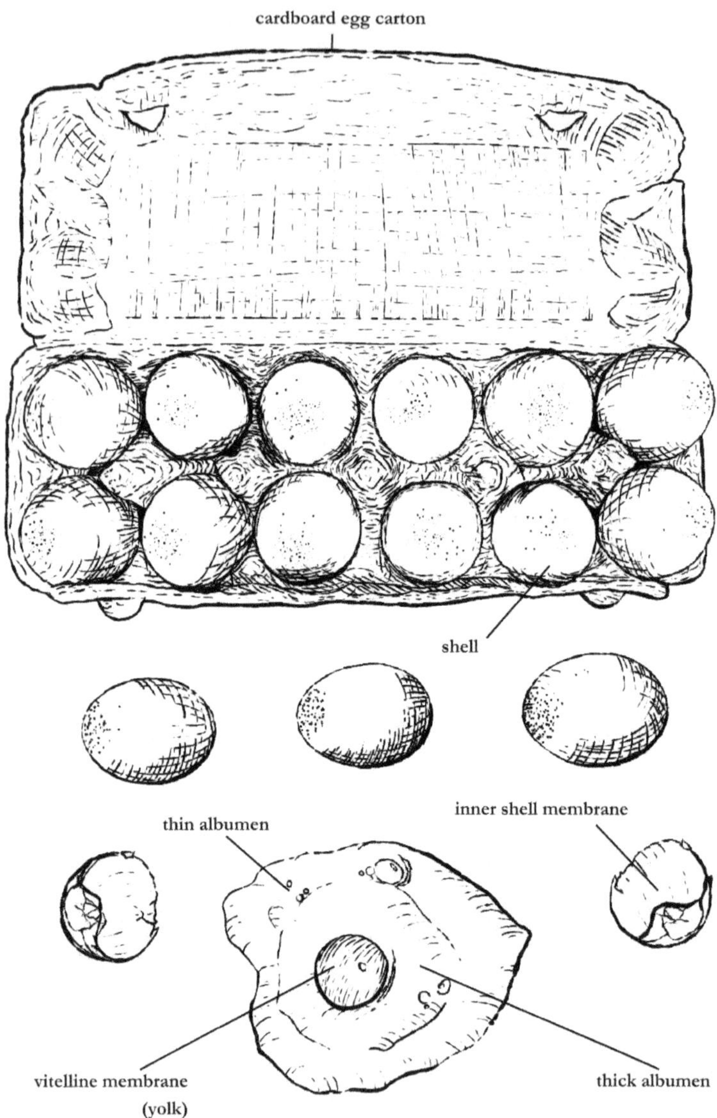
cardboard egg carton
shell
thin albumen
inner shell membrane
vitelline membrane
(yolk)
thick albumen

Eggs

Shannon Lewis

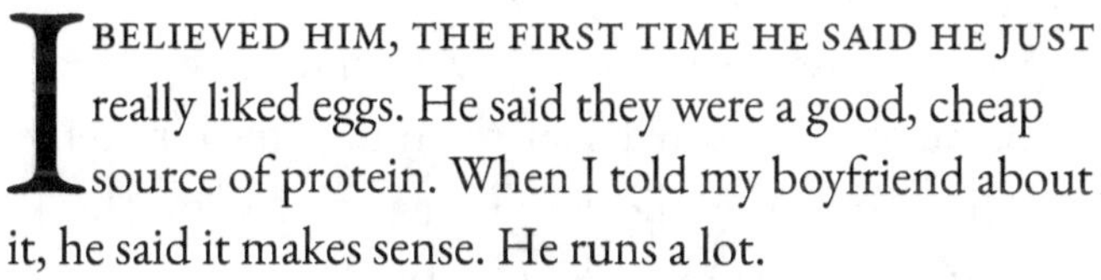

I BELIEVED HIM, THE FIRST TIME HE SAID HE JUST really liked eggs. He said they were a good, cheap source of protein. When I told my boyfriend about it, he said it makes sense. He runs a lot.

I moved in with my boyfriend, officially, in late December. In reality, I had been spending most of my time there since October. His house was nicer than mine: detached, in a neighbourhood far enough from the city centre that it was actually quiet at night, and I was growing sick of my housemates. We had all graduated university at the same time, but the three of them had decided to stay on and do a Masters degree while I had started work as a catering assistant. It was part-time, *for now* I'd tell anyone who asked, but it was fixed hours and I enjoyed it. My housemates all had varied schedules, which meant someone was always awake and the kitchen was always a mess with an "I'll clean it when I get home from class" message left on the house chat.

I used to think there was no real divide between university and otherwise, except in the day-to-day activities, but I soon found myself growing distant from my house-mates. They kept inviting me to plans that less than six months ago I had enjoyed myself—getting a drink at the bar on campus, going on a society pub crawl. I had work in the morning, I told myself and them, that was why I couldn't go out and get obliterated on Snakebites on a Tuesday afternoon. But really, I felt out of place on my old university campus, like the pathetic ghosts of grad-uated seniors that still hit up high school parties. The fewer fun things I did with my housemates, the less I saw them. As weeks passed, they stopped being the friends I'd spent the past few years living with and transformed into the stack of unsorted mail, the funny smell from the closed bedroom door, the pile of soggy clothes that has been sitting in the tumble drier for two days.

My boyfriend's house was a haven by comparison. He was several years older, out of university for nearly a decade, and had been living with the same single house-mate for the past four years. They had established a neat schedule together: the floors mopped and vacuumed weekly, the dish soap replaced when nearly empty rather than watered down for months on end. They both worked around the kind of five-day-a-week-nine-to-five schedule that my artier uni friends reviled.

We weren't dating the first night I stayed over. I had gone over to his for dinner and spent the evening com-plaining about the party that was going on that night at my house. I didn't even have work the next day, but I was reaching my breaking point. He offered for me to stay at his instead of having to make the thirty-minute journey home, to a house I didn't want to be in. They had a spare room they mostly used for storage, but it had a bed and he said he could track down some extra sheets. So, I stayed over. One night turned into two, turned into three, four—I only left because I could start to smell myself on the clothes I was wearing. On night two, I moved from the small box room into his and stayed there the rest of the time. His sheets were crisp and smelled faintly of lavender.

We began dating shortly after. I always teased him that I had started dating him out of convenience more so than anything, but we both knew it was a long time coming. At that point, I only knew his housemate from passing glances. I knew his name was Altan, and that he was out of the house every weekday, but we hadn't exchanged more than fifteen words. From what my boyfriend told, Altan was deeply independent and a little withdrawn, but altogether an alright guy.

When November rolled around, I began making plans to move in. I kept asking my boyfriend to double-check with Altan that it was okay and he would tell me I was there anyway so he was sure Altan would appreciate me paying my share of rent. But the assurance it was going to be fine wasn't enough for me; they had this perfect little ecosystem and I was nervous introducing a new element. I kept pressing it, asking him to get verbal confirmation. By the end of the month, I had found an exchange student to sublet my old room to, had gone for a "moving out" dinner with my housemates (who I had started to like again, now that I was leaving), and received a "he said sure" from my boyfriend. I moved over a weekend.

Instantly, things felt different. When I was staying here as a girlfriend, I felt extraneous, stealing their water, borrowing their kettle, using their mugs. I was an appendix: there, not bothering anyone, but not adding anything. As soon as I moved in, I became a part of their microbiome. I added my collection of cutlery to theirs (meaning we finally had more than three forks), I provided a new kettle to replace the calcium-ridden contraption that had been kicking around since Britney Spears' "Toxic" was topping the charts, and I was paying for bills, too, meaning I could take a shower on my coin.

I knew my uni friends thought it was stupid of me to move in with someone I had only been dating a short while. But I could tell it was going to work out just fine. It had to. And it had. I loved my new schedule. I loved how neat and tidy my life had become, how there was a space for my coat and a different one for my hat, how I had tiny blocks of time to use accordingly. Throughout university, I didn't spend more than five hours at a time alone, between living in halls and housemates and friends and study partners. It was refreshing, now, to have the hours laid out before me like a five-course meal I could eat at my leisure. I used to call people whenever I had to walk anywhere longer than fifteen minutes, but the signal near the house was so terrible, there was no point. Instead, I listened to podcasts on my long walk to work. I was going to have to learn to be alone. Living so far from the city centre meant it was a trek to get anywhere and for anyone to get to me.

After officially moving in, I still thought the house was nice, but I finally started perceiving its flaws. It was an odd-shaped house, for one, pressed against a garage that seemed to take up more space than it actually did. The refrigerator was a bit small, the front door lock had a tendency to get stuck, and if you stood in the back garden, you sometimes got a whiff of something earthy and rotten that reminded me we lived near the neighbourhood compost site.

I now found myself at home while my boyfriend was away. I learned Altan's schedule quickly; it was fairly static. He left for work at seven and got home at five. We talked casually sometimes. I would ask him how work had gone and vice versa, but I would still go through my boyfriend to ask about weightier matters, like when the rent was due, or if I could borrow his clotheshorse. The first time I managed to gather up the courage to ask my own fully-fledged favour was in mid-January. I asked if I could steal some of his salt, because I couldn't find mine. He said sure, I could just grab it out of his cupboard.

We shared cutlery, crockery, and mugs, but each person got their own food cupboard. Mine consisted mostly of rolls of Digestives and packs of pasta while my boyfriend's was filled with interesting spices. I had never seen inside Altan's before that point. The salt was at the very front, but what caught my eye was the multiple cartons of eggs in the back corner. Five twelve-packs stacked neatly meant there were up to sixty eggs in Altan's possession.

I turned to find Altan standing at the sink. He had somehow slunk into the kitchen without my notice. He had a remarkably light foot, especially compared to my boyfriend's elephant steps that thundered throughout the house.

I tried my hand at gentle ribbing, "That's a lot of eggs."

He turned on the tap and began rinsing off a plate, "I mean, yeah, they're really good protein."

I grabbed the salt and emptied a quantity into my hand, "So I've heard."

"You can feel free to borrow one, if you ever need," he said, placing the plate carefully in the drying rack. "Just let me know, so I know to replace it."

"Ah, thanks. I'll bear it in mind." The salt rained into my pasta water, fizzing into the erupting bubbles. The last thing I wanted to do was admit that I would likely never have to take him up on that favor because the meal I was preparing now, pasta with tomato sauce, constituted 75% of my diet (the remaining quarter being made up by plain Weetabix with a sprinkling of sugar).

Altan finished cleaning up his dishes and I put a jar of sauce on the hob, a comfortable domestic silence washing over us. It was impossible not to think of my old house, where someone was always playing loud noughties pop over a speaker and there was never any milk because no one replaced the carton they finished. The water gurgled happily, and the kitchen felt small in a cozy kind of way.

"I really like eggs," Altan's voice was a murmur,

sounding more like a thought spilling out than something said for the benefit of others. When I turned around, he had already gone.

I didn't understand eggs. According to my parents, I used to eat them just fine but one day, when I was around four, I gave up on them completely. I couldn't fathom ever bringing myself to eat them again. They're fine in baked goods, where you can't see or taste them, but the idea of someone just cracking an egg into a hot pan and eating that set off goosebumps along my arms. The smell was the worst. It stuck to the inside of your nostrils, cloying, sulphuric, wet.

I told my boyfriend about it that evening, framing it more like the successful social encounter it was, rather than a critique of Altan's extensive and eccentric hoard of eggs. My boyfriend was encouraging, said he told me Altan was a nice guy and that we would get along. It hardly counts as getting along, I told him, but I was still proud. Somehow, the lightly teasing, vaguely personal conversation had helped me cross the threshold from "housemate's girlfriend" to "housemate." It was a start, at least.

The next day was one of my rare Saturdays off. It was the first full day all three of us were in the house at the same time. My boyfriend and I got up early-ish, had lazy weekend morning sex, and fell back asleep for an hour. We woke up to a light knock on the door. Altan's voice seeped through. "I'm going to the shop. Do you need anything?" My boyfriend asked me if I needed anything and I said I was good. "Could you please buy me some tomatoes and a bulb of garlic?" he asked, before kissing me on the nose. "Sure." Altan replied. I waited for the door slam before I nuzzled onto my boyfriend's chest and asked, "What you making?" "I'm making you homemade pasta sauce."

I made no comment. It was a sweet gesture, and I appreciated it, but I knew before he made it that I wouldn't like it. Sauce from a jar is fine because it is a single thing. If it's one thing then I can fathom it. But if I can see the sauce being made then it becomes parts and I can taste all of them and feel them against my tongue and can't bring myself to swallow.

We spent most of the day in our room, binge-watching *The Great British Bake Off*, while Altan spent most of the day downstairs. We kept the bedroom door open, realising that the room was starting to smell of human. My boyfriend disappeared to the kitchen in the early evening to make dinner. I tasted a bite, trying to keep from spitting it out, but I ended up having to run to the bathroom to dispose of it in a tissue when I bit into a tomato and felt it squelch between my teeth. I came back to the room apologising profusely and tried to explain. I fixed myself a bowl of plain buttered pasta, and our TV binge continued. Altan came upstairs, disappearing briefly in his room before emerging with a pack of six eggs. I watched him disappear back down the stairs, my fork halfway to my mouth. I elbowed my boyfriend and asked in a low whisper, "Why does Altan keep eggs in his room?" "What?" he asked, full volume. I kept my voice low. "Altan just came upstairs empty-handed, went to his room, and walked out with a carton of eggs."

"Huh," He frowned and looked briefly conspiratorial, before breaking in a goofy grin, "Hey Altan!"

I shoved him, but it was too late.

Altan called out from downstairs, "Yeah?"

"Why did you have eggs in your room? It's freaking Nina out."

I could have thrown my bowl of tagliatelle in his face, but Altan called back. "Oh. I just bought some when I went shopping and accidentally forgot them in my room."

"Cool." my boyfriend shoveled pasta into his mouth, "See? Nothing suspicious." "You're such an asshole." I scooted away from him.

"What? You need to stop... walking on eggshells around him." He bit his bottom lip in utter enjoyment at his own joke. I threw a single noodle at him. It landed lengthwise across his face. His tongue flicked out like a lizard's and he slurped it down. I laughed.

Onscreen, Paul Hollywood was explaining that a contestant's angel food cake had fallen flat because they didn't add enough eggs. The next contestant had, apparently, added too many. My boyfriend laughed, "Impossible to please him." I nodded and gave a chuckle, but my mind was elsewhere. See, Altan's explanation was perfectly logical. I've definitely left groceries in my room before, and I knew he'd gone to the shops earlier today, but something about it still felt off. There were so many eggs in his cupboard yesterday. How could Altan possibly need any more?

Weeks passed and Altan and I became tentative acquaintances. He knew I had a sister, I knew the names of some of his coworkers, and it no longer felt uncomfortable when my boyfriend was away. Our friendship was like something placed in increasingly boiling water, cooking slowly until suddenly I realised it was complete. One Thursday, when only he and I were home, I was in the living room reading a book while he was in the kitchen, making himself dinner.

"Come here." I heard him say.

His tone was urgent, almost manic. I padded into the kitchen, intrigued. On the counter he had a bowl, in one hand an eggshell. "Look," he said, pointing at the contents of the bowl, his voice breathy with awe, "double yolk." It was too late for me to turn back. I breathed through my mouth as I peeked over the rim of the bowl. There, floating in a clear slime, were two bright yellow yolks, wet in a way I always imagined organs are. "Cool." I said, trying to ignore the nausea. My mouth filled with saliva and I ended up running upstairs to the bathroom, where I clutched the sides of the sink and wheesed breath.

That night, I dreamt of eggs. The catering work I do is all administrative, so I don't work with the food itself. But in my dream, I was tasked with cracking several hundred eggs into an industrial-size mixer for a massive quiche. Each egg made a hissing noise when I cracked it, as if I was breaking a seal, and, though I tried to keep the egg from getting on my hands, within minutes my fingers were slick and sticky. At a certain point, I was overcome with madness and reached out to poke one of the small yellow yolks. The smooth membrane offered some resistance to my index finger, but I kept pressing and it burst, the golden liquid inside warm as it gushed against my hand. I woke up covered in a layer of sweat.

As the year progressed, a cold settled into the house. The windows were double-glazed, but it was the coldest February in the decade and there was little we could do but crank the heating and hope we would stop seeing our breath inside. The cold messed with the metal fixtures of the house, primarily the front door. The lock became permanently jammed. What I once found difficult to grapple with was now impossible, so I took to going in through the unlocked garage instead, which brought me through the back garden, past the rotten smell of compost, and in via the kitchen door. My boyfriend said there was a way of pulling and pressing on the front door just right, but it wasn't worth the hassle for me.

It was that time of year when it got dark early. I got home one day, coming in through the kitchen door, and thought I'd alighted on an empty house. None of the lights were on, so I felt my way through the kitchen, careful not to knock into the rubbish bin, and found myself in the main hall. From there, I could hear a faint din coming from the living room and followed a pale blue computer glow in. I figured either Altan or my boyfriend had started watching something on the downstairs computer and hadn't gotten up to turn the light on.

Altan was sitting at the computer, eyes glued to the screen, which displayed a video of somebody cracking an egg into a bowl and then hand-whisking it. From the living room door, I could hear Altan take a slow shuddering breath. In each hand, he was holding an egg, turning them over, rubbing them with his thumb. I couldn't bring myself to speak, but I also couldn't move. After a while transfixed, I gained enough presence of mind to try backing out of the room. I accidentally hit the door, filling the room with an unexpected clatter. Altan cried out, his hands tightening into fists that exploded the eggs. He hit at his keyboard with an eggy hand, closing out of the video, then turned around frantically and made eye contact with me. We spoke at the same time. "Hey Altan." "I didn't hear you come in." After a pregnant pause, I answered. "I came in through the garage." He stared at me, yolk running down his wrist.

I dashed towards the hall, mumbling something about going to take a shower, and barricaded myself in my room where I stayed until I heard the sound of an unlocking front door. I crept out of my hideout and waited at the top of the stairs. The house lights were all on, and the darkness of earlier seemed distant. My boyfriend entered and, seeing me waiting, held his arms open for a hug. I ran down to him and buried myself in his arms, aware that Altan was standing in the kitchen, cooking up dinner, watching.

That night in bed, as we lay cuddling before sleep, I opened my mouth to tell him about it. But the more I tried to broach the subject, the less I understood it. After several minutes trying to form a coherent thought, my boyfriend filled the silence with a work story and I jumped at the opportunity for a different conversation. I became absorbed in the new topic and fell asleep without giving the earlier incident a second thought.

Soon, the winter cold was waning, giving way to a tentative spring warmth. The sky was blue as often as it was grey, and I no longer felt the need to wear two jumpers inside. It was light out when I left for work and when I got home. I no longer came in through the garage anyway, but in early March we had the landlord take a look at the front lock and, by the week's end, it was working just fine. I happily spent time with my boyfriend and Altan together but if my boyfriend was out, I kept to our room.

On the first real sunny day of the year, my boyfriend asked me if I liked Eton mess. "Of course not." I told him. "Do you like strawberries?" he asked. "Yes." "Do you like double cream?" "Sure." "Do you like merengue?" "I don't know." He gave me a bewildered look. "Who doesn't like merengue? It's just egg whites and sugar." I shrugged. "I don't like eggs." "Oh, come on, it doesn't even taste of eggs." "Still."

He looked me up and down, his thoughts visible on his face. "Thing is," he said, "Altan makes really good homemade Eton mess. He's planning on making some and I really think you should try it. I think you'll like it." "I dunno." "Trust me. You liked the cheese sauce I made for homemade mac n' cheese that you swore you would hate." "It's liquified cheese. How could I not like it? Besides, it didn't have eggs."

He frowned, "What's your thing with eggs?" "I

don't like them." "You eat cakes." "They're alright in cakes. They're not the main ingredient in cakes." "Okay. Well you liked the custard we had on Christmas." "Sure." "Well that's mainly eggs."

I thought for a moment. "I didn't know that." My boyfriend smiled, "I didn't either until I watched Altan make it." "Altan made the custard?" "Yeah. He's a good baker." I went quiet. There was no way he could know. I shrugged, watching the frustration bubble up on his face. I thought back to Christmas, to the apple crumble we'd eaten at midnight while watching cheesy Claymation films. Altan spent the holidays with family, so we'd had the house to ourselves, spending the day alternating between eating and screwing. I had doused my crumble in the custard I had assumed was store-bought. In my memory, it was sweet and sticky, although recalling it now, I couldn't help but imagine it as thick, heady. Emulsified egg yolks masqueraded with sugar. I don't know what face I made, but judging by my boyfriend's sudden look of worry, I must have gone quite pale. He didn't bring up Eton mess again.

One afternoon in the dead of spring, I came home to a smell that turned my stomach upside down. Initially, I thought it was just the compost site, which had thawed out in the spring sun and smelled stronger every day. As soon as I walked through the front door, I saw it was something else. Eggs. I joined my boyfriend in the living room and asked what was going on. He told me that Altan was preparing Easter eggs for his family reunion this Sunday. He had a German aunt and cousins who loved the tradition, so he always brought several dozen highly decorated egg shells to hide around his grandparents' garden. The American way of decorating Easter eggs, the kind I grew up with, revolves around hard-boiling eggs and dipping them in different cups of food coloring. Altan went more continental Europe, making a pinprick hole on the top and bottom of the egg, holding one end to his lips, and blowing the insides into a prepared bowl. When the yolk wouldn't come out, he would stick the needle back in through one of the holes and scrambled the insides, then blow again. After emptying the eggs, he washed out the shells with vinegar, then used acrylic and watercolor paints to cover the empty shells with colorful patterns. He was good, some of the eggs printed with miniscule chicks and bunnies against the backdrop of verdant meadows, but I felt my stomach turn. Every egg he blew out landed in the rising pile of egg goo with a splat that wafted the scent through to the living room. I told my boyfriend I was going to take a shower. I turned the water slightly hotter than comfortable and scrubbed at my skin with a loofah until it was red and raw.

Altan left late Saturday evening. On Sunday morning, I went downstairs to make some tea and found two chocolate eggs waiting on the counter. One had my boyfriend's name piped in chocolate on it, and the other mine, but they were both almost the size of my head. Mine was milk chocolate, his white.

"Nice, he got you one." I jumped. I hadn't heard my boyfriend join me downstairs. "Does he do this a lot?" "Just for Easter. One of his family members runs a chocolate shop so he gets them for free. Wanna crack them open?" I shrugged, but he didn't notice as he was already tearing away at the plastic packaging. There was something in the milky whiteness of his egg that made it look real, as if waiting inside the chocolate shell was a yolk the size of my fist. He broke his in half and I breathed in sharply. But it was hollow.

He handed me mine. "I don't know if I really want mine." I said, watching him gnash on a chunk of his. "Too early? Come on, I'll make some hot chocolate. We can use the Easter eggs like a cup." I shook my head and he frowned.

"Do you want mine?" I offered. He raised an eyebrow. "Why don't you want yours?" I glanced back at the chocolate dome, trying to imagine it was anything else: a rugby ball, a giant pill, but bile still rose to the back of my throat. "It's just," I said, "I don't like eggs."

I didn't want to look at him, but I could feel him rolling his eyes. "Nina." I used my index finger to scratch at my thumbnail. "Nina, that's ridiculous." "I mean. Just." I met my boyfriend's gaze, noticed a chunk of white chocolate melting between his fingers. I spoke to the space just over his shoulder, "Don't you think Altan likes eggs a little too much?"

He took a second to recover. "It's chocolate!" "It's not just this." "It's Easter!" "It's not that either. I just, what kind of man needs more than a dozen eggs in his cupboard? What kind of person keeps eggs in his room?" "He doesn't keep eggs in his room. I thought that was a joke." "I don't know." I caught my boyfriend's gaze, the crestfallen look of a ruined holiday, and I felt the words die on my lips. I shook my head and fixed on a smile.

"I'm sorry," I touched him gingerly on the shoulder, "it's been a bit stressful at work and I didn't sleep well. I'm being silly." He frowned, then licked the melted chocolate off his fingers. "Why don't you start heating milk up on the stovetop? I'll unpack my egg." He nodded, sulky, and turned towards the fridge. I opened my chocolate carefully and stared at it, unwrapped. I glanced at my boyfriend, moodily stirring at a pot of milk, and turned back to the egg. It was darker brown than most eggs, but that just made it look unnatural. I raised my arm and brought my fist down onto it, cracking it apart until it was just chunks of chocolate. My boyfriend turned around to find out what the commotion was. I offered him a handful of chocolate to melt into the milk, deliberately chewing at a piece, trying to ignore the inward curve of the shaped chocolate against my tongue.

The year got hotter, a record-breaking heat cracking through the unprecedentedly cold winter. The grass thawed out and grew in swathes, although reports projected it would eventually dry up and crumble in the continued heat. The skies were blue, with all the clouds burning away, and the smell of compost grew stronger by the day. It was fine. Altan was going on vacation to Italy for a week. My boyfriend and I, for the first time in months, would have the house to ourselves for an extended period of time, which couldn't have come at a better time. I had been having a particularly bad streak of sleepless nights that made me groggy and irritable.

For the last week or so, I kept startling awake sometime between 2 and 3 am for no discernable reason. The night before Altan left for his flight, I woke up to the sound of an almost papery crack. I laid completely still, straining to listen through my boyfriend's heavy breathing. It came again, soft and sudden. Like someone carefully prying open an egg. My stomach roiled. When I finally fell back asleep, I dreamt that my fingers were covered in something sticky and orange. By the time I woke up, Altan was gone.

The first few days, we celebrated our newfound household freedom the way any couple would: watching TV at full volume until the wee hours of the morning. After hours of directionless watching, we decided it may be worth going through our extensive must-watch list.

We settled on *Rocky*, because he was appalled I hadn't seen it. "We need some movie-watching snacks." He said, grabbing his car keys, "I'll be back." I smiled and settled back into the nest we had built on the couch. But as soon as the door slammed closed, I became unavoidably aware of how alone I was in the house. A joking thought flitted through my mind, wondering if Altan left any eggs behind or if he finished them off before leaving. It nestled in my brain until I found myself heading towards the kitchen to peek into his cupboard. There were a dozen eggs, but the expiration date was weeks from now. That made sense, I told myself, and I was being silly. Then another thought cropped up. Does Altan keep eggs in his room? I was joking, of course— this was just to scratch a curiosity that obviously wasn't there. I climbed the stairs quietly, as if there was someone in the house I was trying to avoid.

I cracked open the door to Altan's room and peeked through. It was neat: his bed was made, there was no clutter on the floor, and he seemed to keep all his clothes in a plain white set of drawers in the corner. I didn't know what else I expected. It was how he kept the house. I opened the door fully enough that I could slip in. Something about the room felt wrong, and it was only once I was stood inside that I realized what it was. Altan's room was a mirror image of my boyfriend's down to the size, shape, and placement of the windows, but the wall that separated them was different. Altan's room had a built-in closet. It was almost hidden, painted the same shade of off-white as the surrounding wall.

I took hold of the handle and wrenched it open, fully prepared to see a few hanging coats and maybe a board game or two. My stomach flipped. Inside Altan's closet were stacks and stacks of egg cartons. From floor to wall, there must have been at least two hundred. For a moment, I wondered if there was some kind of art project he used the cartons for, but that only made sense if they were empty. Skin clammy, I reached out to flip one open to confirm what I already knew: they were full of eggs.

I stumbled downstairs and sprawled out on the couch, my stomach tying itself into knots that it then pulled tight. My boyfriend got home minutes later and made some comment about finding me exactly where he left me. I gave him a grin as he settled in next to me and pressed play on the movie. For snacks he had bought popcorn and peanut M&Ms, my favorite movie combo. But as I held a peanut M&M between my fingers I became aware of its specific shape. I tried bringing it to my lips, but my stomach felt as though someone had smacked it with a white-hot pan, so I let the chocolate fall back in the bag and turned my full attention to the movie.

Rocky was great. A quarter of the way through I made a comment along the lines of "how have I not seen this?" and my boyfriend agreed. We cuddled and the pain in my guts waned, although now it felt like there was something simmering in there. My stomach bubbled and Rocky punched hanging chunks of meat and my boyfriend affected a stupid grin.

Everyone knows about the Rocky training montage. In terms of famous movie moments, it's up there with "I'm flying, Jack" and the Darth Vader reveal. So when the music started up and Rocky put on those grey sweats, I was ready for some classic action. Then Rocky went to the kitchen. I watched Sylvester Stallone crack egg after egg into a cup and, before I could look away, he had downed the contents. My stomach came to a full boil, which set off a searing pain, and I spent the rest of the movie trying to not go full fetal.

"What did you think?" my boyfriend asked, credits throwing light on his expectant smile. "It was good." "Just good?" "Really good." He accepted that, satisfied, then said, "I have a surprise for you."

"What is it?"

He stood up and motioned for me to follow. He

explained on our way to the kitchen: "So, you like pasta. And I like cooking. And I like cooking for you. Ergo, I thought maybe we could make some homemade pasta, because then it's like a 'fancy version' but you still eat it." I gave his hand a squeeze, "That's really sweet." "I found a recipe online. It seems easy enough."

He had the ingredients laid out, including a jar of pre-packaged tomato sauce I knew was there for me. I tried focusing on that, but my eyes were drawn repeatedly to the carton that sat next to the bag of flour. It was only a six-egg pack, smaller than anything Altan usually went for, but it injected me with a full-body nausea.

My boyfriend laid out a chopping board for each of us and piled flour on. "It says you have to be careful not to overmix it," he said, making a divot in the top of his pile, "come on, just follow me. Apparently overmixing activates the gluten." I stood in front of my flour and used my thumb to shape it the same as his. The flour was soft against my fingers, like a pile of dust. My boyfriend cracked an egg into his first, then mine. I stared at the yolk, which seemed to glow a jaundiced yellow, then watched as he used the tips of his fingers to break through membrane and slime. "Nina, you try." I looked down at my egg and reached slowly to touch it. The yolk was slippery against my finger, but I wrenched it away before the outer membrane could collapse. My stomach throbbed. I ran to the bathroom upstairs and dry heaved into the sink. When I realised nothing was going to happen, I sat down to pee and found my underwear was stained a dark red. Everywhere below my ribs felt tender and raw, as if I had spent the last few hours hanging upside down in a freezer being punched by the Italian Stallion.

I told my boyfriend I was on my period and feeling extremely nauseated, so I might skip out on dinner and he said he understood, then teased me, suggesting I had eaten too many peanut M&Ms. I waited for him on the sofa, curled up, trying to block out the gurgle of boiling water. He seemed happy enough with the result, going back for seconds and then thirds. I had missed out, apparently. I smiled at him, surreptitiously breathing through my mouth. Later in the week I carried four packs of pasta from my cupboard out to the bins. I read online that most premade pasta doesn't contain eggs, but they were contaminated in my mind now.

Altan came back and things stayed the same. It was hard to avoid the sensation of blurring edges. My boyfriend worked his usual hours. Altan left the house at seven and came home at five. I was on call most Saturdays. The sound of cracking woke me up most nights, sometimes punctuated by shallow breaths that made my chest tight. Every day the house felt smaller.

One day, my boyfriend announced that work was sending him to France over the weekend to talk to a new client. It was a big deal, apparently. He'd been spending more nights in the last few weeks tapping away at his laptop after hours.

He asked if I wanted to come with, but of course it was the weekend and I couldn't get time off. Besides, I told him, he was going to be busy working the whole time. We could plan a more deliberate trip to France over the summer, when my holiday hours reset. "I'm really happy for you," I hugged him tight, trying to maintain my veneer of normalcy.

He left on Friday with no more than a backpack and told me he'd be home soon. Saturday morning, I let my alarm sound for longer than I usually did. I went through the motions of getting ready, careful to slam the front door on my way out. I took a walk around the neighbourhood, enjoying the way the brick houses were outlined against a sky that was a fragile shade of blue. I doubled back after an hour, figuring that was enough time. I had booked this Saturday off the day my boyfriend told me he was leaving for the weekend. I'd had enough. I wanted to understand, to confront Altan, but I knew he would never outright admit anything. I'd have to catch him off-guard.

I came in through the garage, sliding it closed as quietly as possible. As soon as I emerged into the back garden, I was hit with the stench of rotting. The compost pile smelled like a corpse. Before I could sneak in through the kitchen, a soft squelching sound caught my ear. I surveyed the garden and noticed nothing out of place, except the smell that glued itself to the inside of my nose. I sniffed the air, trying to follow the trail of the wafting scent. I found myself on the side of the garage, where there was a pathway blocked by a few slats of wood. I moved them and squeezed into it, edging along until it opened up again. The squelching was loud now, obvious, and the smell of compost thick in the air.

I emerged to find a small plot appended to our property, probably intended to be an herb garden. It had been turned into a pool of sorts, a hole dug into the dirt that was just about chest-deep. To prevent leakages, the edges of the pool had been lined with pale white and brown flakes of material no bigger than a penny. Eggshells. Inside the pool were thousands of eggs, wobbling in the breeze, some black with rot, some freshly cracked. Altan sat in the pool, clearly naked, making direct eye contact with me. He had a few cartons of eggs on the side and he cracked one in, then another, then another. I backed away, through the tight path along the side of the garage, until I was back in the garden.

I looked up at the sky. Eggshell blue with clouds of membrane white and it seemed to me the sun looked like a giant golden yolk. A calm had settled over me like I had never felt before. For once, I could perceive the components as a whole. I entered through the kitchen and opened my cupboard. Waiting for me was a pack of six eggs. I pulled it out, then grabbed a glass from the drying rack. I cracked in one, then another, then another, and more until there were none left in the carton. The yolks swam in the egg whites like the globs of a lava lamp. I up-ended the glass into my mouth slowly, swallowing twice, feeling the yolks burst at the back of my throat until my insides were coated in slime.

Fig. 10 — axe

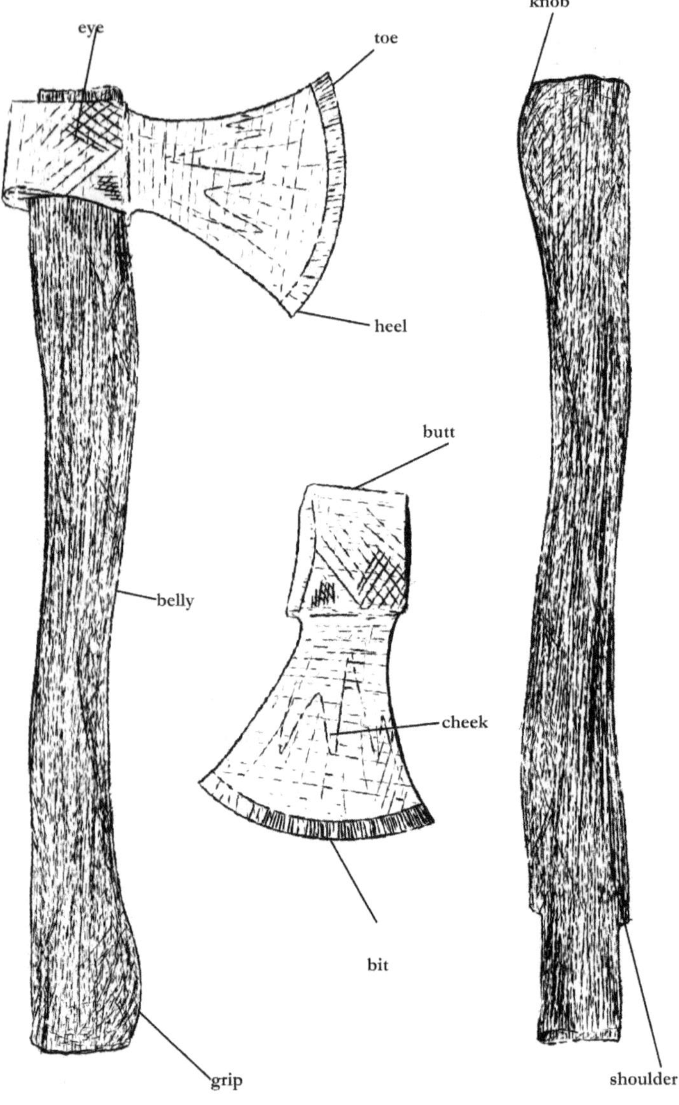

Kill Your Youngest

Kathryn Leigh

NOW IMAGINE FOR A MOMENT THAT YOU are the mother of twelve children. You live on a farmstead miles from town, the water is frozen in iron pools in the hoofprints and ruts. The sky roils with unshed snow and a cold unlucky wind tears the leaves from the trees. In the warmer months, the deer living in the woods fed and clothed you all, but now following the cloven prints leads your family on a days-long hunt for nothing. The fields bear only gravel. The snares are sprung but empty, or with a single frostbitten limb of bird or hare hanging within. Not enough to feed even a ghost. You sleep, only to see in your dreams your own mother's mother.

How will we survive this winter?

Kill your horse.

And so you do, but he is more bone than flesh, and now the cart's wheels freeze to the earth, hoar frost jagged on its stiff reigns. Your family eat gruel from horse's oats and ice. There is frosted lace on the inside of your window and the logpile grows low. The bones of the horse boil in the pot, turning over like driftwood in shallow waters, and the broth cannot quench your hunger anymore. It tastes like weeping.

How will we survive this winter?

Your mother's mother looks grave.

Pray to the devils.

And so you pray to the devils. You have nothing to offer them but your wedding ring. Is misery what devils eat? So you've heard. They laugh around the chimney all night, they frolic in the shadows cast by the embers. Your husband wheezes in his sleep when you return to bed.

At dawn, you bury yourself in furs and stagger in the direction of town. Begging from those with the foresight to live within the walls will be easy after what you have already endured. Pride evaporated with the fat of the horse. You make it a mile on the treacherous ground before the air is too cold to bear. Your fourth finger on your right hand, where the wedding ring used to be, refuses to bend anymore. When you try to make your retreat, the devils turn the wind and drive the snow directly into your face. It takes twice as long to return as it ought to. Your family still hides in the bed. Your husband's teeth chatter. Your children's hands are purple. The pot and its hearth are empty.

How will we survive this winter?

Kill your youngest to feed the others.

My youngest to feed the others?

> *Your youngest to feed the others.*

Your mother's mother has a devil's face. You have heard the word infanticide. But you think of Abraham, and how in righteousness he held a knife above his child's throat. Your tears fail to bring warmth to your numb face.

In the morning it seems the birds refuse to sing. The small fire you build in the hearth shrinks back. You fear your own children—what if they should turn on you, murder you in return? How to disguise the flesh of their sibling so they do not recognise their own blood in their hungry mouths?

(More terrifying, perhaps, the prospect of this inspiring the older to kill their parents in greed.)

Your youngest child is small and pale.

It is time you learned to cut wood, you say. You take the child's hand, bluish, birdlike. You lead her from the house to the stable, where the axe stands propped against the useless cart. You show her how to sharpen it with a whetstone.

So sharp, you say, *that it could cut your skin.*

The child's fingers are cautious around the blade.

Hand-in-hand you walk towards the edge of the wood. Since the winter drew in, your sons have been cutting trees by the road, not wanting to venture into the realms of starving wolves. You head in farther. Behind you, the orange light of your hearthfire is just visible. The child hangs behind, the axe in her hands. It's heavy for a child, but you don't trust yourself not to cut her down in the open, be done with it, and let your family watch you do it from the house—two distant grey forms in an act of violence. You'd be hung in the middle of town.

How far to go? She asks in a whine. The axe is leaving a trail in the snow.

You snatch it up and walk on.

And here, a clearing, for summer tree-felling. The pines stand close, like cowled saints, casting pointed shadows dark across the ground. The tree stump in the centre is weathered and damp, criss-crossed with axe marks from vicious or misaimed blows.

Go stand over there.

She is obedient.

Pray to God that we survive this winter.

She kneels. The axe feels heavy, like dragging a person from water.

But mama, don't we pray to the devils?

It casts its grey shadow on her white neck.

But mama, don't we pray to the devils?

Silence. The wind picks up, the child turns to see mother with raised axe in white-knuckled hands.

Don't be afraid.

She runs.

You lunge with the axe and it rattles your bones as it thuds into the frozen ground. She is gone. You chase, she twists through the trees leaving footprints as small as a deer's. You curse, you hear your own panting breath, hot on your throat, a cloud that you breathe and shatter with each stride. The child is a white rabbit's tail bobbing just out of reach.

You think you hear the wolves howling. You swipe at the air, scream at a crow that crosses your path. Your mother's mother's voice rails at you, *kill the girl, and all will be well, kill the girl and you'll dine like kings.*

You trip and fall, rolling over the axe, and you see on the path ahead a wolf, dead, frozen, opened, and bloody. Wolves are not the hunters in the deep forest. You howl for losing your child, and keep running. The trees flash past in an endless reel, each tall, each black, the foxes yowl. You come upon footprints once again, and follow them round to a clearing with an axed stump and a child kneeling.

You wheeze for breath, stumble forward, dragging the axe behind you.

Silence, like that in an untouched cave, an unused mausoleum, in the crowd before the hanged man drops.

It is night, your breath steams. The child sits in clear air. She uncouples her hands, and raises her head. The axe is so heavy. You take laboured steps.

Your child has your mother's mother's eyes as she watches a point beyond your shoulder. You think of your house, no food and the hearthfire crackling.

Kill the others to feed your youngest, she says.

Do not be afraid.

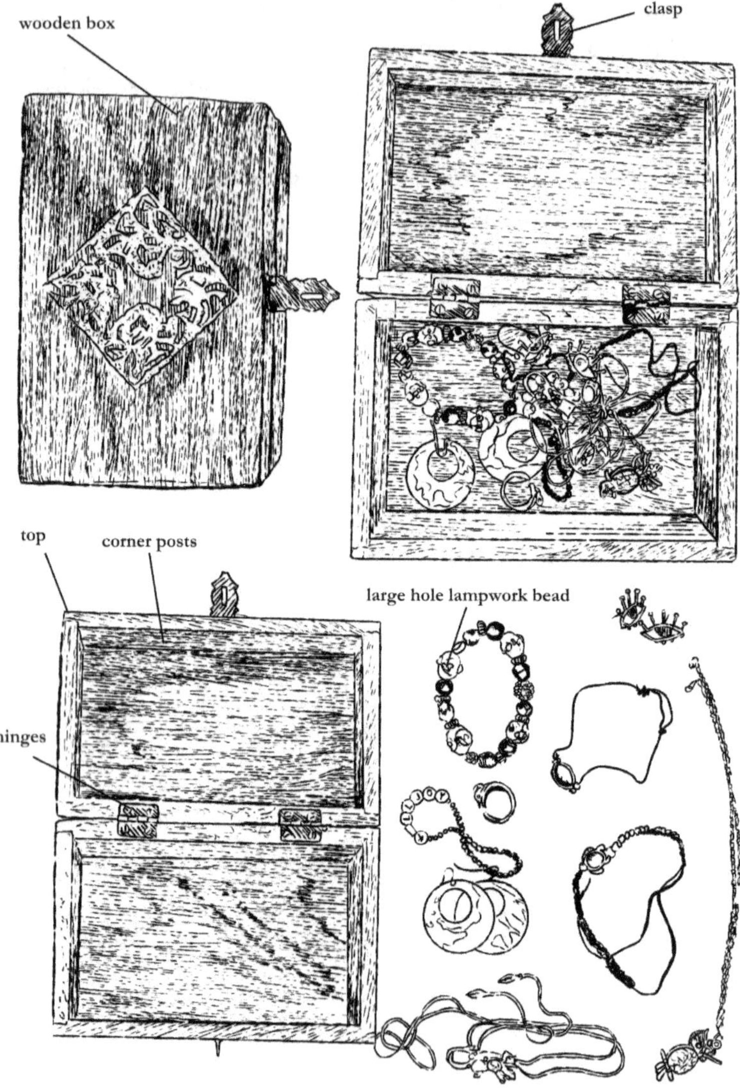

Fig. 11 — jewellery box

Spaces

Georgina Pearsall

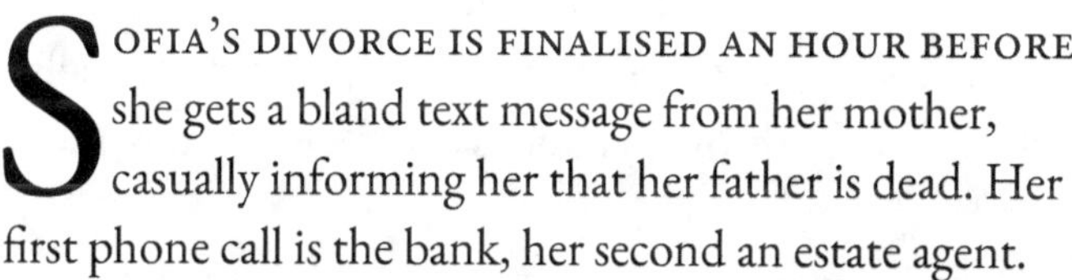

SOFIA'S DIVORCE IS FINALISED AN HOUR BEFORE she gets a bland text message from her mother, casually informing her that her father is dead. Her first phone call is the bank, her second an estate agent.

The flat is brand new. It's most of why she chooses it, loaded down with an excess of income following the open wound of her divorce. The surfaces gleam and, on signing, the estate agent ask her to do a personality quiz to test her suitability at thirty-four years of age to keep up with all of the trendy young professionals.

Her new neighbours eye her with suspicion. She's an occupying force. They haven't seen her at the conferences or the rooftop bars. She looks like she might bring a child into the building, or—God forbid—a cat. She's in in two weeks, using the cover of moving to skip the funeral.

The moving company she hires fills the flat with her mismatched belongings, one half of a life together. A partial dining set filled in hastily with cheap extras. A sofa without its matching armchair. A king-sized bed with a double duvet that hardly meets the corners of the mattress. The warm woods of the carefully selected antique pieces clash with the smooth metal surfaces. Dale hadn't fought her for anything, and where she thought she'd picked the best of it, the results look more like a supermarket sweep. The over-large furniture encroaches into the sleek, open-plan spaces, ripped from a country manor house tucked up against the Norfolk coastline with a garden and a sea view and a grade two listed certificate. The flat looks more like her university room, the last space she decorated alone, with framed prints from movies she's not sure she's seen leaning against the walls and a colourful throw that looks cheap despite the price tag.

She could, of course, have gone home. But after twelve years of marriage Sofia found she had no hobbies and very few friends. 'Family' is up north, and the years of cohabitation have seen her meander further and further south, drawn first by education and then work and then Dale until the march of progress has left her alone in this over-priced flat to die. Their home is his now. Even if she'd wanted to fight him for it, the place is tarnished with his affair, occupied by his new girlfriend, and stuffed full of his dreams for the future. No kids, thank God.

The Thames squirms around the building, dark green and murky, shifting up and down the banks with the tides. Eerie, especially given the stark contrast of the clear blue swimming pool protected under a greenhouse roof below her. She can watch people swimming below her, like pond-skippers skimming along the top.

The flat is a short drive from her office. No one knows much about her. She's been part-time and strictly work-from-home since she got engaged and Dale quietly paid her student loans behind her back. She's an accountant, ever the straight man to her husband's artistic career, the maths student, the sober one at every Literature party Dale brought her to. They've agreed to a trial-basis return to full time and in-office. It's client-based, it's monotonous. She's still somewhere towards the bottom of the ladder. She can rebrand, be married to her job. She might not like her job, but she hadn't much liked her husband, either.

On Saturday, Sofia ignores three calls from her mother and two from her younger sister, whose wedding she's three weekends away from blowing off. She's laying in bed staring at the ceiling as the last of her compassionate leave ticks out from under her—a divorce, a move and a death in the family, you poor thing. She's spent most of it on Pinterest and Instagram trying to pick out a new aesthetic and a new personality at once.

There are two bedrooms at opposite ends of the flat. The south wall of the flat is a long stretch of glass, high enough from the ground for the illusion of privacy (even though there are half a dozen other buildings at the same height that must be able to stare in). It has two en-suite bathrooms, which it's hard not to find ridiculous. The estate agent had apologised for the lack of a third general use bathroom. She'd thought about being a kid, growing up in a house with seven people and one bathroom, then told the estate agent that it was obviously a disappointment, but she might be able to make do. Her bedroom comes with a small balcony where she hides an ashtray from the cleaners who come bundled with the flat, part of the maintenance fees. The effect of it all is to make her feel just a little like a zoo animal. She tries to hold onto her dignity inside of her enclosure, but she's all too aware that even if the mattress is new, she's on the bed frame where her husband spent two years having sex with his PA.

On Sunday, she's setting herself up to piece together a work wardrobe from tennis club outfits and country pub outfits and work-from-home outfits, lifestyle You-Tubers echoing in her head. She's curled up in bed with coffee, bracing herself for the return to work, carefully not thinking about Dale and how blindsided she had been by his eventual confession. She's plotting an outfit that will make her look strong. A trouser suit, a slightly risqué blouse, pointy stilettos that say "Partner" more than they say "Assistant Analyst." Things she shouldn't be able to afford on her meagre salary.

Then, a bird flies into the perfect glass of her balcony door and collapses dead onto the concrete.

It makes an ugly cracking noise and reflects back and forward over and over again between the glass door and the glass railing. She watches its twitching death throes, frozen in surprise. After what feels like an hour, Sofia creeps up to the window, pressing a hand against the door and staring at it, hoping it might reanimate and fly away.

A drop of blood drips down the glass. When it becomes apparent it won't move, she unlocks the door. Her fingertips leave marks on the glass. Errant feathers blow around the balcony. It's a parakeet, another neighbourhood invader, with its neck bent at a right angle.

She digs through the kitchen for a carrier bag and scoops it up, walks with it at arm's length to the building's rubbish chute, swallowing a gag. She pulls it open and holds the bird over the gaping hole. Catholicism creeps up on her. Her dad would've buried it. Said something about the dignity of all creatures, even as he pulled dead mice out of their traps in the grain store. She drops the handle and it slams shut, the bang reverberating around the empty hallway.

Diving back into the flat before she's spotted—the cleaners always seem to be roving around the immaculate hallways—she empties the tiny broken body onto her antique coffee table. She digs around in the spare room, looking at as little as she can. She finds a pair of embroidered MR & MRS hand towels and the jewellery box from their wooden wedding anniversary. It makes her feel a little sick now, knowing his assistant certainly picked it out and set the calendar reminder for him to give it to her. She tips the contents, costume jewellery from her university days, into the top of a cardboard moving box and swaddles the bird in a MRS towel before tucking it into the jewellery box and closing the clasp.

Her toolbox was lost in the move, folding trowel included. It was the first thing she'd tried to find—there's a flatpack chest of drawers half-assembled in the spare room. In the end she finds a shiny stainless steel serving spoon.

With the box in her hands she rides the lift down to the garden. The whole place is deserted, but she still feels strangely observed with the towering glass.

It's unnerving, suddenly, to know that she has to make all of her decisions alone now, carry them out alone, feel the consequences alone. If someone were to stand with her and indulgently go along with her as she digs down into the soft dirt until she hits gravel a foot and a half down, she might feel better about it.

She nestles the box into the fresh hole, drags the damp earth back into place with her fingertips.

"I'm sorry you died on my balcony."

Sofia flattens the earth back down, drawing a wonky cross with the blade of the trowel. She expects to feel better, but the dread that washed over her at the sound of the bird's feeble little body colliding with the glass has dug talons into her guts. She mumbles some Latin, half Oxford education and half lapsed Catholic, and wonders who spoke at her father's funeral. Wonders when the catharsis comes. There are two parakeets up in the trees. One gives a squawk that seems—nothing.

Then her leave is over. The dread clings on, but she takes herself to work anyway. It's strange to be back in the office where she has to be a physical presence rather than just an extra screen in a Teams meeting or an email. She feels exposed, over-visible. Yet almost no one talks to her. She's older and fatter than the last time she was here, and much less vital. The sad divorcee. Even though her boss knows she's coming in, he still gives an audible "Oh," when he sees her before he catches himself. "It's just so strange to see you in person. I almost forgot you had legs!"

He makes the team introduce themselves in a circle, tell-everyone-a-bit-about-yourself, as she moves from being a name CC'd on department emails to a person again. It's uncomfortable and, flailing, she tells them about her new flat, how perfect it is, how wonderful it is after the hallowed halls of her marital home.

It's still better than another day in the flat. The silence of the empty kitchen-diner is somehow louder than the bustle of hot-desking colleagues and tea runs. At least at work she sees a glimpse of who she could be again, who she was before she was shipped out to the countryside with Dale's antique typewriter and smoking jacket. His first book came out nine months after they got married, and his star rose quickly from there.

Every day that week, she makes it home just in time to miss the flat's cleaning service. She parks in the underground garage, her ridiculous countryside estate car not built for London life, but her dad called it sturdy, reliable, something he wished he could've had at her age. He loved driving it so much she used to put him on the insurance when she visited. It would be quicker to walk or get the Tube than it is to sit in traffic, but this way she can go from the underground carpark here to the underground carpark at work without having to set foot outside.

She wonders who would be called to identify her body as the lift rises. There's no next of kin listed on any of her documents anymore. Would he come down from Norfolk, cast an appraising eye over her withered corpse with a solemn nod? Would her mother make the drive, still in funeral blacks, weeping as she stares at the body of a daughter she hasn't seen outside of photos in two years? Would her siblings come down together, the four of them huddled around her in tatty clothing? Would anyone know what to dress her in from her scattered wardrobe? She tries and fails to shrug smoothly out of her jacket. It's tighter on her now than it was when she bought it, but too expensive for her to part with.

She hangs the jacket by the door and walks straight into the sofa.

Her knee slams into the oak frame and her toes curl up underneath it, shunting her toenails back into her cuticles. Sofia shouts. There's plenty of room for the sofa to tuck up against the end table, but somehow the cleaners move it every single time and leave it overhanging the hallway. It's become a symbol of something, the first piece she picked out antiquing that Dale approved of and the first thing carried into their first home. She shoves it, not without spite. Pushes it back into the corner. Then she straightens the coffee table, tilts the armchair back to where it belongs, facing the empty television stand, and straightens the two chairs at the four-person dining table. It's too big now, for the space it and for her life. She bites back a sharp, irrational urge to kick it.

With an assessing breath she looks around the space. The few pieces of art she took have turned out to be prints, her eye not trained enough to tell the difference. Dale would drag her to auction and spend thousands on pieces she thought looked dreadful until she saw them hung and lit. The floor is still rug-less, the huge square floor rug from her old living room too costly to wrap up and ship. It wasn't an absence of money, it was the sound of her father's voice in her head, ever presenting monetary figures in terms of how many weeks of food or rent they would buy, how any hours of labour would have to be observed to cover it. The underfloor heating leeches into her feet.

The following weekend she goes shopping as if in a dream. It's a hollow effort to quiet her father's voice. When they got married, Dale angrily defended his decision not to have her sign a prenup to his parents. They were soulmates, after all. In the divorce he barely fought, busy starting on his new life with his new soulmate, and as a consequence she's laden down with an amount of money that makes her feel itchy and shameful. Not exactly earned, by her or by him, probably not by his parents either, a swelling supply of capital that dragged her with it.

His third novel had just sold and he'd split every penny of their (his) savings down the centre, even though his "income" had covered the house, even though he'd paid off her student loans, carried her through the low-salary years of chartering as an accountant, looked the other way for years as she guiltily posted cheques to her mother. He's moved on now, and if the price of getting her gone fast was half of his estate he'd happily paid it.

The shops around the flat fit the new image—high-flier, independent, strong. She drifts around looking at replacement crockery (twelve hours' work) and cashmere throws (a month's rent). She makes it to Selfridges and is asked for her ID over a bottle of week's-worth-of-food-for-a-family-of-seven wine, with the bratty seventeen-year-old behind the counter acting like it should be flattering. It's less flattering when the manager gives her one look, rolls her eyes, and tells the cashier that she's obviously over twenty-five. Sofia resists the urge to buy a corkscrew and drink it on the way home.

She circles around Selfridges, then Hobbs, LK Bennett, ends up in Zara. She lists home and drops the bags on the coffee table to survey the damage and is shocked to find they're almost empty. Her full day of shopping has amounted to a four-pack of long-handled teaspoons, a lint roller, a photo board, a throw pillow that doesn't go with her hateful sofa, and a tiny gold foundation compact. There's at least a decent small rug that she lays out on the living room floor. It looks like it shrunk in the wash. She finds herself laying on it until she spills the wine trying to drink on her back. The stain spreads slowly, pooling out like blood on the pale fabric.

Everything else stays on the coffee table until bedtime, when she sweeps it into a Zara bag and drops it in the spare room. For a moment she could swear something chirps, and she closes the door in a slam.

The spare room remains a graveyard of boxes, stacked on top of the sofa bed and shoved in around odd pieces of furniture she can't fit into the open-plan spaces. Most of her kitchenware is still in there somewhere, leaving her eating off of her wedding china and cooking everything in a wok. She refreshes his Wikipedia page while she eats one-handed, waiting for someone to update it with their divorce. She looks at Rightmove to see if he's selling yet.

Then it's two weeks later. She's late to work, really for no reason but complacency. She'd been staring at her new ceiling. It was completely smooth, plaster less than a year old. Their house had been full of Artex ceiling in big swirling patterns. He'd hated them, called them tacky and old-fashioned. She'd argued in favour of keeping them. They reminded her of his parents' house, the confidence of old money, not the ever-shifting always-dated attempts at modern living her mother threw around her childhood home while her father rolled his eyes fondly and helped her unfurl wallpaper rolls. It was always Sofia's job to hold the bottom of the roll as the shortest member of the family.

When she arrives in the office, there's an email at the top of her inbox asking her to come to a meeting in the small conference room at 9:30. There's no subject, and she's late enough that she only really has time to drop her bag and coat before she walks over. One of the juniors asks her if she wants a posh coffee as she bustles past, and Sofia smilingly digs her out a handful of cash and asks for an oat milk latte.

Her boss is waiting when she makes it to the meeting. She's starting to pull optimism back out of the depths, along with a bubblier version of herself that makes a joke about traffic. For a moment she thinks she's getting good news, a promotion, an office, a raise. Then the HR Manager and her boss' boss arrive behind her, and she knows she's made a mistake.

Her boss is three years younger than her. They went to the same school. She hates him.

"We're undergoing a re-structure, and there's just no need to have you full time. The company is offering voluntary redundancy," says Helen (not a natural blonde).

"We think it could be a good opportunity for you. Your progress here has stagnated a little," says Mark (obviously hems his own trousers).

"I would be delighted to recommend you," says Christine (expensive manicure, cheap shoes).

With a promise of more money than her father made in a year, she's handed a box of her things, her coat and her handbag, and escorted out of the building by security. It doesn't occur to her to make a scene until she's in her car, blinking at the carpark exit, wondering how to get out without her pass. It swings open smoothly anyway, anticipating her departure.

There's a "Sorry to see you go" card in the top of the box. Everyone knew before she did, and no one thought to warn her. She doesn't remember her latte until she's parked at home.

Isabelle, one of the cleaners, is still there when Sofia

gets in. She's about the same age as Sofia's mother, with two kids and three grandkids and a tiny, terraced house in east London she's lived in forever. She talks while she's cleaning whenever Sofia is home without really needing to be prompted or responded to, for which Sophia feels absurdly grateful. It saves her from having to do what Dale would have done (smoothly ignore her) or what her mother would've done (die of shame any time a speck of dust is discovered, leave with all the village gossip). She's cheerful.

"Oh, hi Mrs Lee, I wasn't expecting you back," Isabelle smiles, "I'm just finishing up, unless there's anything else you need? I'm sorry I'm not sure I'm going to be able to get that rug back to pristine, I can recommend a good dry cleaning service though, they might have more luck."

She's dusting, using a long pole to get into the corners of the high ceilings.

"Did a bird get in here? I found some feathers under the coffee table. Quite a few, actually. It seemed strange so high up—do they really bother to come up this high? It's not like there's anything to eat in here. Do they allow pets in these flats? I suppose they can't stop you when you own. I'd be lost without my..."

Sofia dodges around the furniture towards the second bedroom, biting her tongue as she bumps her hip against the sofa.

"Short day," Sofia explains, "I should—I have to put this down."

Isabelle politely looks away as she opens the door to

the spare room. With the box in her arms she can't see where she's going, which is why she stumbles, tripping on the box pressed against the door. In fact, all of the boxes are up against the door. It's impossible to get into the room; they're stacked to her shoulders. She knocks a few off the top as she collides with the cardboard. The noise makes Isabella start, look over. Inside, she can see that a number of them have been torn open, ornaments broken, furniture butted up against the boxes. It looks like someone has picked the room up and turned it on its side, then let it drop back to normal.

She drops the box she's holding. An "I Hate Mondays" mug rolls across the floor.

"Are you oka—woah. What happened here?" Isabelle stands behind her, duster in hand.

"What?" Sofia starts slowly, before she can shake her way out of shock, "what do you mean? You're—you're the only person who's been in here, I've been gone all day, what did you do?"

"What?" Isabelle mirrors, putting the duster down, "Mrs Lee—"

"Ms. It's Ms, you know it's—it doesn't matter, I—you should leave."

"Ms Lee, none of the girls go in there, you asked us not to bother when you moved in. I'm sure we can get to the bottom of this, why don't you sit down? I could make you a cup of tea, you seem like you've had a long day—"

"No. No, no. Get out. I don't need cleaning staff I—I can do it myself, I just. Leave."

Isabelle nods, gives her the pitying look of a parent watching their nap-deprived toddler throw a tantrum. "I promise you none of the girls did this. You have my number for when you calm down."

Sofia realises she's shaking. The front door closes. She rubs her arms, staring at the mess, which looks insurmountable. She can't even get in the room. There's guilt, too, bubbling. She almost goes after Isabelle to apologise. Her mother used to clean houses to make ends meet when she was little. Sofia would go with her sometimes. The older, cynical part of her wonders if she should get Isabelle back just to make sure she hasn't stolen anything and the guilt tugs noose-tight on her intestines. What would she take? There's probably jewellery in here somewhere. It would make sense if there was jewellery; she dumped out a handful of it to bury the bird. Was there art? Did he take that when he left? She feels sick.

Making the mess worse, she shoves a few more boxes off of the top of the pile until she can climb over and get into the room. She picks up the pieces of half of a tea set, sweeping the broken porcelain into a little pile with her hands and scooping the pieces into a box that was laying on its side. There's a mix of old books and CDs, a wooden box of love letters. The box is from him, the letters aren't. She reaches further into the mess and pulls her hand back sharply, watches blood drip from her fingers onto the carpet. It soaks in, spreading out through the pale grey fibres. It's her father's beer mug, a gift from her. Hand-blown with his initials etched into the glass, the only fancy thing she'd ever gotten him to actually use. Even then it was only because he'd never known how much it cost. Someone must have shipped it back to her.

With little success, she spends thirty minutes trying to scrub blood out of the carpet. She should call her mother, ask what to do for blood. She finishes clearing up the boxes, half unpacking and half repacking. Her wedding ring is moved to the bathroom counter, a carefully boxed set of champagne flutes into the kitchen. Her childhood teddy bear is held, considered, and packed away with her university work and her graduation photos. She comes back across the family photos, pulls the album out and sits on the rug in the living room. Brushing a hand over it, she notices there's no stain. Isabelle must have managed it after all.

The first Christmas he attended at hers he looks miserably out of place. They're all in polyester jumpers, stuffed into their tiny front room. Her brothers and sisters are grinning with a motley crew of partners and children hanging around, her parents squeezed into the centre. He had offered to take the picture rather than be in it three times. Beside him her family looks scruffy. It was the first time she'd seen the house through someone else's eyes, and she can't help but look at the old-fashioned carpet, the chipped paint on the mantel, her father's yellow smoker's teeth and her mother's cheap dye job. He's wearing a cashmere jumper. Her oldest niece is in the front row, covered in chocolate.

The next year she's at his parents' house, lined up on the staircase with a professional photographer arranging them. She's in a dress she bought on a credit card she couldn't afford to pay off and she's beaming. As the years go on, her clothes stay expensive, but her smile is more subdued. Casual. It takes her years, but she learns to match the quietness of his family, copy his mother's manners and put away her own. He never joined her family for Christmas after the first one, always made an excuse and sent her up with a Selfridges hamper and a promise about next year. After a few years she stopped going too, stayed with him and his parents for champagne breakfasts and dressing for dinner.

She shoves the pictures back into the box, covers them in a tablecloth, and puts it at the back of the room with two boxes stacked on top of it, like she's weighting it down. There's a thump from the bedroom that has her rushing out to the balcony, but there's nothing there. The city thrums out of earshot below.

The next day, she's half moping and half luxuriating in her silk sheets when she's woken up by the landline phone ringing in the living room. It's unfamiliar, which makes it jarring, and it rings off once only to start ringing again. She crawls out of bed with her duvet still wrapped around her shoulders to answer it.

"H'llo?"

"Oh, I didn't expect to catch you at home." It's her mother's phone voice, a slightly more clipped and high-pitched version of her usual Northern drawl. "Is everything alright, baby?"

"Mum," Sofia drops the duvet and reflexively stands up straight. She worries at the cut on her hand with her thumbnail. "No, it's uh—the office. Shut today. There was a power cut so, working from home. Sorry, I know I sound distracted I uh—I was in the middle of a report. How are you?"

"Oh, that's dreadful—I didn't realise that kind of thing still happened, London is so fancy. I hope it's sorted soon. But anyway, I was going to leave you a message, I don't think you've set up your machine. You remember, it's Maisie's youngest's birthday this weekend? Evie? I don't think you've seen her in—oh, it must be three Christmases at least. You should come home. You know, now you're alone. It'll be good for you. You can go and see your father's plot."

Sofia nearly chews through her bottom lip.

"Yeah, I—that sounds great, obviously." It doesn't. "I wish I could make it." She doesn't. "It's just I—god, I can't believe I forgot to mention this—the office is sending me to, um," Sofia forgets all of the nouns she'd known mere moments ago. "To a conference. Overseas. It's, uh, Singapore? So this weekend is just too short notice. I'll send Evelyn a postcard, try and pick her up a gift." She braces her hand on the marble counters, real, at least six grand's worth, cool and solid. Steps into the bedroom.

"Of course." She hates how easily her mother accepts it, especially when she was so unconvincing. But adults aren't allowed to call other adults liars. "How are you coping, love?" Sofia drifts onto the balcony, watches the swimmers under the glass roof absently.

"I'm so sorry—I have a call on the other line. I'm

still at work today, technically. I'll call you back."

Sofia hangs up before her mother can say anything else and drops the phone like it's on fire. Feathers are blowing around the balcony, sticking together like a damp green tumbleweed. One sticks to the side of her foot, yellow, speckled with blood.

She walks into the armchair as she circles back to the living room to put the phone away, hisses in pain as her toenails list away from the nailbed. She shoves it in retaliation, kicking it with the heel of her good foot and sending it rattling backwards. An antique wooden leg snaps, and the expensive monstrosity that's adorned at least three generations of middle-class homes stumbles backwards and comes to rest in an awkward lean. She stands poised, as if she's waiting to be attacked again. It hardly seems to fit in the place, now, like the walls have been pulled in on her.

His mother gave her the chair. She'd taken her own mother to visit his family while she was staying down south, and her mother had been so effusive with her praise for the thing—just like the ones Sofia's grand-father used to make in his little shop—that Eloise had given it to her when they bought their house, along with the deposit and a set of monogrammed towels. It was probably worth close to a thousand pounds. Her moth-er sent them an embroidered pillow with "home sweet home" on it and Sofia put it in the third guest room. He took it in the divorce.

The flat seems to shrink further in around her as the days creep on. There are coffee cups piled by the sink with takeaway boxes and the wrappers from pre-packed supermarket salads and sandwiches. A cleaner shows up once, but can't get in with the door double locked, and clearly spreads the word.

She unplugs the landline in case her mother calls back.

The place has no history. Not like her Norfolk coast manor with Dale, full of other peoples' lives. At first that was desirable, but now it feels unnerving. It's show-home pristine. There's none of the rattling, creaking and clanking of her previous homes. It is modernity embod-ied with soundproof windows and hardwood floors. She can see the wind beating through the trees until their branches are nearly touching the ground. Cars are bustling around, people are loitering and smoking and chatting, but everything is in mime. She's too high up to hear it, too trapped behind the glass. She's in the only flat on this floor, the penthouse, the rest of the space taken up by an unloved little roof garden too cold to sit in. No one passes by her front door.

When she would actually need a job is complicat-ed. Her money is smartly invested now, with stocks and bonds and annuities and assets held in trust, it would take a better accountant than her to pull it all together and tell her when it might run out. It could be ten or two hundred years for all she paid attention. Her marriage has started to feel like a dream, or like sleepwalking, like someone else was doing it. She writes up an impressive CV with ten years of embellished accomplishments and applies indiscriminately to any job not requesting a cover letter, from CFO to waitress. Her inbox fills with emails requesting more information and she deletes them as fast as they arrive. The next time she opens his Wikipedia, she's listed as his ex-wife.

As if to cement her absence, the old house has gone onto Rightmove. He's obviously hired or bought more furniture, refilled it so skilfully it's like she was never there. There's no documentation of her failed experiment in marital bliss. She clicks back further, finds the photographs they looked at when they bought the house. It looks colder, empty of furniture. There are chips in the paint, the wallpaper is sagging. His parents had called it a solid investment, steeped in history. As if it was always a good thing to be steeped in history, as if her own history hadn't been shameful. He had always loved to tell people about her poor upbringing at Oxford dinner parties—and did you know Sofia's father was a Farmer?—like it was an interesting anecdote, an amusing trivia titbit. She finds the house's previous owners on Facebook, and finds that they're also divorced, smiling out of her screen with new partners and new addresses.

She goes back to the land registry pages, the original blueprints, with a sick feeling in the pit of her stomach. It's Victorian, 1828 with memento mori touches leaking out of the foundations. There's no concrete way to know if someone is buried on the land. The far side of the garden backs up against the village church, the cemetery brushing up to the edges.

It twists up in her gut. The house has been the site of, at a rough count, four affairs, six divorces and seven deaths. There's too much dust lingering around. She chews on the skin around her thumbnail, picking at it until it starts to bleed. Every step she walked in that house traced a path walked a hundred times before.

The flat gleams around her, seeming impervious to dirt. New build. Definitionally, it has no past. Her hands steady on her keyboard, she exhales. She's ready to put it down, stop wandering from room to room with her laptop balanced in the crook of her arm.

But what about the land?

Over the next week, it sets off a new bad habit, a nervous tick to replace the old ones. It keeps her from biting her nails and pulling out her eyebrows. There's no life in the flat to generate dust, but if there were, it would be settling thick on the spaces outside of her bed. She looks for a house with a perfect history.

She starts off with new builds, but they have their own set of problems. The land is never new; England is too small. It's always a farm given over to housing, or demolished buildings. Mental hospitals and old houses, blocks of flats and offices. It feels like the problems of all of the old addresses have seeped into the soil, crept up the foundations into the brickwork. The farm had been in their family for three generations, something that made her dad so proud she cringed at the memory. She was young when they sold it, not familiar with words like gross profit and tax burden and deficit. There was always dirt under his fingernails, his accent was unshakeable and close to impossible to understand if you didn't come from the right part of the country. Her ex-husband was prone to nodding and smiling, like it was all so quaint, all so charming if you didn't have to live in it.

The property search is loosely punctuated with cleaning and sorting. A few things come out of the boxes. A mirror she can't remember the origin of. Cleaning supplies, books she hasn't read yet. But progress is slow; she retreats as if burned whenever she stumbles upon something that draws her too close to the past. Her wedding album is in there somewhere, her wedding dress. The scant and precious supply of childhood photos in a crumbling scrapbook, another box of costume jewellery from her parents she can neither wear nor part with. Her first degree, her childhood stuffed bear, a chipped plant pot taken from her grandmother's house when she died. Sofia reopens the cut on her hand by accident and pokes at it with her thumbnail, watching the blood gather in her open palm. The room still seems to be getting smaller, or the stain bigger. It's almost paradoxical: the more she takes out, the smaller the room becomes.

Dale texts her asking if she knows where his easel is. As if the last text he sent (ignored) wasn't an offer to go to the funeral with her, from when he found out about her father. She didn't even go to the funeral. She wants to scream, she wants to get in the car and drive to their old house, she wants confrontation. She's haunted, stuck, too aware with every move that she's just a short entry on his Wikipedia page.

She finds a house in Cornwall. Its history can be traced back two hundred years to when it was first built. It's expensive, but the seller has spun a beautiful backstory for the property, five generations. She reads it all sitting on the floor of the spare room, back pressed up against a box of shoes. She was looking for her toolbox again, but it's nowhere to be found, and she's already opened two landmine boxes. There's not a speck on the family's record, good Christians, happy marriages and healthy children. Then, when she checks the newspaper records, she discovers that the entirety of the surviving family died in the house, a carbon monoxide leak on Christmas day. She drops her phone, groaning.

She gets up and thinks about going out, only to crash into the sofa. It knocks the wind out of her. It's blocking the entrance to the spare room, backed up against the door. Sofia drops to the floor and scrambles for her phone, dials for the police and then hangs up. Bile rises to the back of her throat. What crime has been committed here?

"Hello?"

There's no answer, no sound. The cupboard doors all hang open, the windows are flung wide, wind whipping through.

She climbs over the sofa, stands on it to shut the door behind her.

She turns back at the sound of her name. It's coming from the spare room, soft and echoing. She walks out of the flat, grabbing her car keys, and takes the lift down to the carpark. Chewing on her thumb, she gets into the driver's seat of the car and grips the steering wheel. There are birds singing.

When she looks in the rear-view mirror, she realises

there's a toolbox on the back seat. It's an old metal box, well-loved, large and heavy and overflowing. Her father's initials are painted on the front. He was so horrified when he realised Dale didn't have one—why would he have needed one? Fixing things was someone else's job—that he packed them one out of his own duplicate tools the same day.

She turns off the engine, then picks up the toolbox and walks back to the lift. The flat is how she left it, for better or worse.

She's being ridiculous, crazy; she can get past all of this just by taking a deep breath and living like a normal person. The toolbox is a heavy weight at her side. She drops it on the dining table. The table is safe; she bought it with the flat. The chairs are dangerous. She stares at the toolbox while she makes dinner. The white walls swell and bulge when she looks at them for too long, almost completely unadorned. The silence of the flat is impossible to trust. She stares at her wedding ring as she brushes her teeth and her insides twist and twist. What had she been thinking bringing it all with her? What use is a fresh start if you drag your past with you? Sofia lays awake all night.

It's a rainy Friday morning. The sofa should go first. It's too big, old and ugly. It doesn't fit now anyway, overhangs the doorway even pushed flush to the wall. The coffee table isn't straight where the rug has been dragged, and the armchair is practically offensive. Rain beats against the windows, soundless. She tries to see her makeshift grave, but she's too far away. She wonders if the rain will wash it out. She wonders who will clean and sweep her father's grave.

She starts out with a screwdriver, but the furniture is all old, put together by carpenters relying on wood-working joins and glues more than metal screws. She starts over with a kitchen knife, a crowbar, and a saw. She finds her old house keys in a cushion as she shears it open with her knife. The legs come off the coffee table. She stamps on the centre of it, splitting the wood in half, and she gathers it like folded paper into a bin bag.

The feet come off of the armchair easily. With enough force, she can snap the back off just by bracing herself against the wall and pushing on it with her legs. The arms are harder work, but with the crowbar jammed underneath she's able to rend it into pieces, separate cushions from the frame and get stuffing all over the floor. She fills two more bin bags with the pieces and rolls the rug up, shoving it into a bin bag and taping everything shut. She half drags, half rolls them out into the hallway. The sofa menaces from the centre of the room.

She makes a clean sweep of the kitchen, tossing everything with a memory attached into a bin bag. The wedding china shatters, so she double bags it, dropping in the "World's Best Wife" mug and the tea towel signed by her pre-school class, her mother's cookbook and her best pan. She takes down the art she has managed to put up, letting the glass break until she's crunching it underfoot. She bundles up the bedding she brought over from the old house, drags it into the hallway.

Then she moves onto the spare room. Nothing is

sacred. For a moment she considers just setting the whole room on fire. She tips the boxes out roughly. Things break on contact with the ground, and she snatches up anything and everything that could tie her to any version of herself that existed before this exact moment in time. She can hardly see what she's discarding, most of it still wrapped in bubble wrap and brown paper, but the photos go, her wedding dress, the letters from her parents, birthday cards and congratulations. She takes the key to her mother's house off of her keyring and drops it into the box. Sofia finds all of the sentimental jewellery she displaced for a dead bird and scoops it up with a plastic bag, refusing to touch it. There's a best friend necklace from her sister. A locket from her grandma. A bracelet from her dad. She will make these people distant strangers; she will erase any traces. She will keep the phone unplugged forever, change her name, fake her death. Anything to get out.

It takes hours. After a while the anger and the fear and the nausea give way, and it becomes mechanical, medical. The spare room is empty. The walls are all bare. The kitchen has cabinets and drawers open; there's still glass and stuffing on the floors. Feathers shuffle around in the air currents.

With weary resignation and the last of her spite, she starts on the sofa.

The cushions are sewn into place, a smooth upholstery job in one large piece of fabric. They chose it together, the first and last thing. She guts it, starting with the knife and ending with her hands, pulling off fabric and stuffing cotton and horsehair into a bin bag. The mahogany refuses to break when she kicks at it, stamps on it, throws her weight into it. So she reaches for a larger saw, cuts it inelegantly into odd-sized, choppy pieces. Finished, she bags up the tools as well. She puts her wedding ring in with her family photos.

She leaves the living room in pandemonium, takes the last of the wine to bed, and sleeps restlessly. She can hear her parents in her head. Such a waste, terrible be-haviour, we don't throw things away in this family.

The next morning when she opens the door she's braced for guilt and mess, but the living room is empty. Every bag is gone, the furniture, the shattered glass from the floor. It's just her and her clean, unmarked walls. The smooth, low ceiling. Not a speck of dust.

The flat is almost bare, her wardrobe decimated. The only furniture that's left is the small black-top dining table, the new bed in the spare room, the new mattress from her bed. Her down quilt is gone, but there are two cheap pillows left and the polyester duvet from the spare room. Her mobile phone rings in her hand and she throws it off the balcony.

She repeats her old shopping trip with more deter-mination, more needs. With her flat emptied out, she can recommit to being a new person with no history. She's no one. As people watch her walk around, they have no reason to question her, no way of knowing the depths of her failures.

Sofia finds her way back to Selfridges. Christmas is drawing nearer, and there are children everywhere. Posh and squalling and dressed more expensively than she is. Sofia was twenty-seven before she could walk into a place like this without feeling self conscious and embarrassed, and these kids in peacoats won't ever know the feeling of being out of place, an intruder, an imposter. It twists her into knots until she could spit bile at the next nanny-raised blonde-haired under five she sees.

She starts grabbing things without discernment. New dishware. An empty photo album. Silverware. Someone at a counter helps her place a new sofa on order, indulgently expense, too large for anyone's living room and wrapped in smooth black leather. A new bedframe is paid for with even less thought, a television stand in a modern, brushed metal finish. The shop assistants are happy to guess who she should be next. She hides her wince, tamps down on the guilt as she hands over her credit card. They call her ma'am and offer to have everything delivered so she doesn't have to carry anything home. She leaves empty-handed and anxious.

On her way to the door, there's a little girl. She's maybe five years old, clinging to an over-priced wooden reindeer and trying to get her mother's attention. She's crying—big, pretty, rehearsed tears over this stupid, ugly reindeer that isn't even a toy. Without pausing in her step, Sofia snatches it out of her hands. In the crowd and the girl's outsized reaction, no one sees her slip it into her inside coat pocket.

She walks out with it and drops it into the first bin she sees on her way home.

When she unlocks her front door, she notices her

keyring. Her dad gave it to her when he dropped her off at Oxford in a borrowed car. A smooth metal tube with a twenty-pound note rolled inside, fifteen years old and never opened. For emergencies. Always enough for a taxi home. Key still in the lock, she rips the keyring off and drops it in the hallway.

The sight of the flat in the dark is startling. She remembers the show flat they'd showed her, stylish mirrors and art prints and expensive furniture, a life she could just have walked into and pretended to have had all along. Now she's been affecting the space for barely a month, the image is stark and bare, nail marks on the walls and hardwood floors that look cold but remain warm to the touch. It's still spotless, clinical.

She tucks herself into bed feeling nauseous. The mattress feels less plush with just the floor beneath it.

There's this house in Kensington that's been in the same family for three hundred years. It's only available because the current occupant is marrying a foreign prince. It looks well-loved and homey. The address produces no crime reports, just house and country magazine articles and Garden of England awards. There's an aviary built onto the back, full of brightly coloured birds she doesn't recognise.

She sits up abruptly. Someone has called her from the living room. For a moment she thinks it's Dale, then she thinks it's her father. She opens the door to peek, but the room is empty.

Sofia sends the estate agent a message to ask if anyone has ever died there. The estate agent answers immediately, offering to call her. Her phone is gone, but she closes her laptop, makes sure the landline is still unplugged. It's then she notices her degree, still framed on the wall. It sends a shock of pain through her body. She pulls it off the wall and drops it down the rubbish chute in the hallway, listens until she hears it crash to the bottom.

The house looks too empty. It makes her fidget. The clean lines. Around her it sounds like it's breathing. Lying with her mattress on the floor she can almost feel it rise and fall, like it's some large and dying creature she's stepped inside of. She puts a hand on the warm floor, scratches her nails along the wood. The nail of her index finger splits and cracks, and she chews on it absently. It gets dark quickly.

Shifting, Sofia realises there's something hard under the mattress. When she lifts the mattress to check, she finds a hammer with her dad's initials painted on the handle.

She drops it off of the balcony. When she walks into the bathroom her wedding ring is on the counter. From the living room the phone starts ringing.

Sofia stands perfectly still. His voice calls from the living room. Her father calls her from the balcony.

Her wedding ring leaves indents on her hand that threaten to bruise as she clutches it in her fist. She walks out of the flat with her eyes closed. In the carpark she drops the ring down a storm drain.

That night she sleeps in her car.

When she wakes up, her phone is in the cupholder,

ringing.

She stamps on it until it shatters.

Maybe she shouldn't be looking in England at all; maybe there's a distance far enough from here where she ceases to be herself, where she stops being traceable.

The sky is black when she opens the door to the flat. There are storm clouds roiling over the river.

In the centre of the empty living room is her wedding ring, perched atop her jewellery box. Next to it, laying open, is her father's toolbox. There's the grim and grubby photograph of them all; she doesn't remember when it was taken. They're all laughing.

The landline is ringing. Her phone vibrates in her pocket.

She sinks to her knees in front of the makeshift shrine. Her wedding dress is spread over the sofa behind her.

Sofia reaches out a shaking hand and takes her wedding ring. It slides onto her finger. It still fits, even though she's not the same person. The jewellery she poured out of the box, the locket, the bracelet, is all spread out, radiating from the centre. She puts on every item until she gets to the centre.

Before she opens the box she already knows what's inside.

When she opens the lid, the parakeet flies out, chirping, and lands on the back of the armchair.

Fig. 12 — sunscreen

Slow Burn

Shannon Lewis

IT BEGAN AS A TINGLING AT THE BASE OF MY throat, right where my collarbones protrude. It wasn't an itch, but I kept scratching it, something I only noticed when my friend asked me why my neck was red. I wrote it off as allergies, hay fever even though we were at the height of winter, and she had no reason to doubt me. I had no reason to doubt me. If I stopped thinking about the itch that wasn't an itch, it went away.

I started the week with plenty to distract me anyway. My parents called on Monday to ask how housesitting was going and if I'd managed to keep the place from burning down so far. On Tuesday, I did laundry, nearly spilling bleach all over my hands but managing to catch the bottle by the handle at the last minute. Wednesday, my friends and I were supposed to go to the beach, but the sun came out unexpectedly and we didn't feel like fighting the crowds. Sunny days in midwinter turn the waterfront into a firefight. Finding myself alone on Wednesday, I flicked a movie onto the sixty-inch television in the living room and settled in for a lazy weekday.

There was a rumor going around that I'd quit my job at a major tech company on ethical grounds, especially after the scandal that broke about their ill-sourced cobalt, and I'd done nothing to dissuade it. The truth was far more boring: I was an overpaid yet dispensable cell in a spreadsheet of layoffs. I had plenty of savings and the job market had, so far, turned up dry, so I wasn't too concerned. It was a chance to finally get through my long list of must-watch movies.

I didn't notice I had started the scratching again until I got up to go to the bathroom and saw beads of blood along my neck, as well as long pink scratch marks. The surrounding skin was the color of an overripe watermelon and felt hot to the touch. I ran water over a towel and dabbed it into the skin, feeling a hiss of relief. I needed to be more careful, I thought, as I retrieved the nail clippers from under the sink.

As soon as I returned to the living room, the tingling began in my back. I shuffled in my seat, rubbing the fabric of the sofa against my skin, but eventually had to give up on my movie day, finding the sensation too distracting. I took my bike to a local coffee shop, ordered an iced coffee, and scrolled through social media for an hour on their outdoor patio. Eventually, the sun became too much for me and I rode my bike back home. I touched my face and, before I even looked in a mirror, knew it was the telltale pink of a sunburn. We had a large supply of aloe vera in our medicine cabinet, so I sloughed plenty on my face, chest, and shoulders, cursing myself for wearing spaghetti straps. It stung, but only slightly, and I ended up falling asleep in a sticky mess on the downstairs sofa. When I woke up, I was covered in flecks of dried plant matter. They flaked off when I touched my face.

The rest of the week was unobtrusive. It was only on Friday afternoon, when Beth rang up to ask if I could cat-sit for her that I realized I hadn't left the house since the coffee shop. That was bad, I chided myself, as she began listing Panko's allergy medicine schedule. When she paused to breathe between explaining his evening schedule and morning feedings, I interrupted with a deeply apologetic tone. I wouldn't be here this weekend, I was so sorry. But I hoped she could find someone to take care of him. She said that's alright, that she could ask a neighbor. Before she could ask me what my weekend plans were, I told her I had to get going to pack up and she hung up with little resistance. I leaned back in the chair with my phone on my stomach.

I spent the whole weekend in the house, entirely blaming Panko and his ridiculously long list of requirements, chancing only a quick trip to the local grocery store to get chocolate milk and boxed mac n' cheese, lest a mutual acquaintance see me and the information somehow reach Beth that I had stayed in town. Monday was marked by a call from my parents, this time informing me that they had decided to extend their holiday by a week, having struck up a friendship with a vineyard owner who had offered them room and board. They asked if I minded house-sitting a little longer and I told them I was happy for them. They had always wanted to go to Italy and had earned this. I could keep an eye on things here. There was a worried pause in my mom's speech before she asked me how the job hunt was going. Great, I told her, I had an interview lined up for Tuesday and was expecting a phone call on Friday. She brightened, and told me how proud she was of me. When we hung up, I trundled towards the fridge and ate the mac n' cheese leftovers cold, straight from the Tupperware. The congealed cheese sauce stuck in my throat. As I used my index finger to wipe up the last smattering of sauce, I noticed how dry the skin of my knuckles had gone. It was an inflamed red so intense it led me to wonder whether I had eczema. It extended from the first joint of my fingers to the bottom of my knuckles on both hands and itched painfully. In a wave, the sensation on my collarbones and back returned, extending down my front all the way to the tops of my knees. I leaned against the refrigerator, taken aback by a wave of nausea, and wondered if maybe a steady diet of boxed macaroni and premixed chocolate milk wasn't the best choice for a twenty-nine-year-old.

Tuesday, I had planned on venturing into town first thing to pick up some lotion and real food. But I was kept up all night by an intense sensation on my hands that burned away the possibility of sleep. I spent most of the evening with my hands under my pillows, pressing into the cool sheets, flipping the pillows when they grew warm. Only after raiding my parents' medicine cabinet, cringing around the prescription bottles of blue pills and expired tubes of face cream to find and swallow a hand-ful of sleeping pills leftover from my dad's hernia surgery, was I able to finally get some rest.

Bleary-eyed, I managed to drag myself to the store by midday. I ran into Beth, who began to excitedly tell me about her romantic getaway but soon stopped with a worried look on her face. She asked me if I was okay and I said I hadn't slept well. Without prompting, she held the back of her palm against my forehead. Her skin was so cool against mine it was dizzying. You're burning up, she informed me. I took it as an opportunity to tell her that I was pretty sick, had unfortunately had to cancel my weekend away, and felt terrible because I meant to call and ask if she still needed help with Panko but hadn't managed to get far from bed. She raised a hand in a dismissive gesture, said Panko managed fine. She told me to get some fluids and bed rest, and disappeared to finish her shopping.

The skin on my hands started to throb, so I beelined for the pharmacy. I asked the woman in the white coat if she had anything for eczema. She gestured at a selection of creams, some of which needed a prescription. I chose the strongest stuff available to me in the moment, paid at the counter, and left.

I was halfway home when I realized I had forgotten to buy food. I paused, considering my poor, battered bank account. The sun beat down on my flushed skin, making my eyelids feel flimsy as rice paper. It was fine. I could get takeout.

As soon as I was in the house, I unscrewed the cap on the lotion and smeared it onto my skin. It tingled cold, like water after a mint, different to the sizzling pain I had almost grown accustomed to, and that was enough.

I turned the pack over to read through the ingredient list, tiny font and words I didn't even know how to pronounce. Paraffin triggered a memory at the back of my mind. I think they used to make candles with it.

I caught a glance of myself in the mirror on the way back to the sofa. My sunburn was far worse than I had initially suspected. The pale pink was slowly settling into a deep burgundy. My skin was sensitive, sure, but usually it took several unprotected hours to get to this point. This was something else entirely. I usually made fun of my mom for carrying around a lipstick tube of SPF 15, but it seemed I needed to reassess my priorities. My lips were bone dry, flecks of red blood caked into the canyon cracks. I smeared some of the thick white lotion on them, wondering only once it was slathered over my mouth if the product was toxic.

The day burned away like a sheet of paper in a fireplace: slowly at first, then all gone in a blaze. I set up a movie, but couldn't sit still to watch it, the itching coming back to haunt me whenever I laid against any surface. Eventually, even my clothes felt too much and I began removing layers until I was pacing the living room in my underwear. I tried to run a shower, but kept messing up the temperature, every tilt of the dial turning the water either scalding or gelid. I dipped as much of my hand as I could bear into the running water and did a quick clean of my underarms and crotch. It was my first shower, I realized, in around a week. Disappointment clawed at me; I'd promised myself I wouldn't let this happen again. I crawled into bed completely naked, the winter air pulling goosebumps out of my skin.

Despite my horrible sleep schedule, I was wide awake. For five minutes, I let myself lay there, pretending I was deep into a coma. We were a few streets off the main road, so only the occasional car passed by, rumbling past the sound of crickets. I gave up when a siren pierced through the tenuous peace and reached for my laptop.

I opened Google and typed in "leprosy symptoms," using the entirety of my mental fortitude to keep from scratching the top of my hand. The skin there was now a thick crust of flaking layers. I scrolled through several websites, clicking past anything that was too lengthy. As it turned out, leprosy in the modern day was rarer than I expected. Still a shitty disease, though. It wasn't painful or anything. The opposite problem, actually. You lost sensation, especially in your extremities. If you didn't check yourself every few hours, you could lose a toe or an arm to an infection that had camped out without you even noticing. Shuddering, I flipped open a forum of people with leprosy answering questions. This led me down a rabbit hole of strange medical diagnoses, which led to strange scientific phenomena, which eventually led me to an online article that said, because of deoxidation of our cells, the reason humans die is we are technically slowly being set on fire by our atmosphere. I trawled the comments and found everything from enraged claims this was a hoax to horrified responses to scientific explanations as to why this was an oversimplification. My hand kept reaching to scratch the back of my neck or my stomach.

A message popped up on the bottom of my screen. It was from this guy I began talking to months ago, when I had a brief moment of madness and downloaded a dating app. He asked me if I was going to be around our hometown for the holidays because he'd love to see me. He still thought I was in New York. I opened the message and answered that I unfortunately wouldn't. Work was really hectic that time of year. He sent me a broken heart emoji and I responded with a sad face. Only then did I realize how late it had gotten.

My collarbones and my back and the front of my legs all at once began to itch or tingle, I still couldn't quite find the right word, ants crawling under the skin, the feeling of pressing frostbitten fingers against a scorching radiator. I knew I shouldn't scratch but couldn't help myself; my body was no longer fully under my control.

I slammed my laptop shut, tossing it onto my bedside table. It took several minutes of rolling around to realize there was no position where the sheets touched neither the skin on the front of my torso nor the back. They felt remarkably cold, almost painful, the way water against a sore tooth feels like acid. I don't remember falling asleep, but I must have because soon enough I was opening my eyes to a sunlit room. The curtains in my room are thin, lilac, and in dire need of replacement. My brother took the blackout curtains with him when he went off to university last year, so I'd spent the last few weeks rising with the sun. Rather, I'd spent the last few weeks being woken up at an ungodly hour and pulling my blanket over my head to compensate.

The sheet that tangled around me was soaking wet. The fabric clung to me, covered in an off-yellow stain that felt oddly thick. Maybe it was the combination of the lotion and my sweat, like the way deodorant turned shirt armpits ochre. As soon as I thought about the lotion, the itching came back in full force. I pulled myself out of bed, a process that took more effort than expected. When I was finally disentangled of the blanket, I saw I had left behind a ghostly layer of skin stuck to the mattress.

When I was young, my parents took me to a water park. I wore this one-piece swimsuit that had a diamond cut out of the back. My parents managed to wrangle sunscreen onto most of me through the day. My nose, shoulders, my legs. They made it through the day unscathed. My back, though, it hadn't survived as nicely. By the time we got home, there was a perfect diamond painted in deep red right in the middle of my back. I had to sleep on my stomach for almost a week. The third day, I began shedding. Swathes of skin peeling off, papery sections the size of my hand. Rather, I should say, I was peeling it off. At the time, I'd thought it was fun. If I was going to get sunburnt, at least there was an interactive element to it. It reminded me of slathering my hand in wood glue and waiting until it dried.

I stared at the husk I'd left behind, trying not to picture chunks of my skin carved out in perfect diamonds. My breath tasted ashen and my throat was dry. I rushed for the sink and began to swallow water by the handful. Only when I had gulped enough to make my belly distend did I look up at the mirror. I almost screamed. Staring back was someone almost entirely unfamiliar. My hair, which had always run on the thin side, looked like hay. When I touched it, it was scratchy, strands breaking off under my fingers. My arms looked odd too, thinner, as if someone had suctioned a part of them away while I slept. The bones of my forearm bumped up against my skin. I could almost see the ligaments move when I wiggled my fingers. The ends of my collarbones jutted out the sides of my shoulders at awkward angles. I shook my head and searched through the cupboard under the sink until I found my leave-in conditioner. I heaped a glob into my hand and pressed it into my hair. It crunched under my palms.

The lotion was waiting for me where I left it in the living room. I finally read the instruction label, skipping past a yellow warning label, and saw that it said to keep away from eyes, ears, and mouth. It also promoted its new and improved tube design, now providing six months' worth of applications. Mine was already half empty, squeezed thin in the middle. Still, the itching had started up again, pins and needles now a sting, so I began to layer it over myself. My legs and back felt lumpy, the bones ridging up under my skin in places I didn't expect it. I realized I still hadn't put clothes on.

The effort of my attempts to moisturize had exhausted me. I collapsed on the couch, panting, leaving a greasy body print on the fabric of the sofa. Years of use molded the sofa to fit a different body than the one I currently inhabited. How many times had I sat here to study for an exam, to watch violently colorful cartoons? There was a sofa I left behind when I gave up my apartment in the city, a sleek hard thing that looked catalog-ready even after two years.

I reached for the phone I had left on the coffee table. Its battery was low, less than 10%, but that was enough to make a call. The touch screen was slippery under my fingers as I tried to unlock it. No matter how much I tried wiping my fingers off on the sofa, it still wouldn't respond to me. It soon became an untenable mess of iridescent finger tracks. I lobbed it away with a grunt and laid back. There was a phone, I reminded myself, in the kitchen. Dial phone.

I groaned and waited a moment, gathering strength. This was probably nothing. I just had a rash and a fever and it was making me cranky. I rubbed my eyes, remembering too late the warning on the lotion tube. The corners of my eyes began to sting and my vision blurred. I swore and used the burst of annoyance at myself to stand up. As soon as I did, I was hit with a wave of nausea so powerful I threw up on the living room carpet. I dry heaved for several moments after, leaning my hands against my knees to keep from keeling over.

I straightened up and began walking towards the kitchen, mouth sour. Halfway there, my left leg spasmed and I almost toppled onto the floor. Steadying myself against the wall, I waited for the twitching to subside. The leg shuddered, then contracted up into a tight weave of muscle. It felt like vacuum-sealed meat. I reached with one hand to massage it, but the arm that was steadying me decided in that moment to give out on me. My head slammed against the wall, leaving behind a speckle of blood. I couldn't keep waiting. I lowered myself down onto my hands and knees and crawled the rest of the way, my leg dragging behind me like dead weight.

Only once the kitchen phone was in my hand, pulled out of its cradle by the chord, did I realize I didn't know anyone's number. I considered going back to the living room for my phone so I could raid its contact list, but the journey here had been hard enough. I dialed 911, figuring this, whatever it was, had gone too far. I was put through to a dispatcher who asked me what my emergency was. When I spoke, my voice came out raspy, as if my larynx had been beaten thoroughly with a hammer. I cleared my throat and tried again. Explaining that my skin was very red and itchy and I had a fever. Before I could even get into talking about my leg, the dispatcher asked me if I had any allergies. I said no, not that I knew of, but that I had been in the sun recently. The dispatcher asked me if what I had was a sunburn. I blinked. There was silence on the line. I swore I could hear someone in the distance laughing so I said, more angrily than I expected, that my leg was also not work- ing. The dispatcher asked me to explain and, to the best of my ability, I told her what had happened in the living room and about the lotion. She still seemed skeptical, but she told me she would dispatch an ambulance. I gave her my address and thanked her. She told me someone was already on their way and to just stay calm in the meantime. Dial tone. I let go of the phone. It swung by its chord like a hangman.

Stay calm, I told myself. Calm. The itching had stopped, but I hadn't noticed when exactly that had happened. Instead there was a pain emanating all over my body, a high crackling sting that was nothing like a paper cut and everything like accidentally touching a hot pan. When I poked my thigh to check the muscle, my finger pressed against something brittle and dry like kindling. My heart rate quickened and I could feel black seeping its way into the edge of my vision. Stay calm, I told myself. I looked around the kitchen. My eye landed on a stack of empty mugs piled next to the sink. Tea. Tea was calming.

I dragged myself along the floor until I was sitting by the sink. I reached up for the nearest mug, my fingers just able to reach the top of the counter without getting up. I hooked my index finger around the handle of a mug and brought it down to inspect its contents. It was mostly clean, only a thin layer of sediment caked to the bottom that was probably the remnants of an old cup of tea anyway. The tea we kept in a cupboard near the ground, so that part was easy enough. Heating it was where I would find a challenge. The microwave was so high up there was no way I could reach it without standing and standing was impossible. My right leg had started along the same path as the left. Only my right arm really seemed to be in working order. My breath quickened and the room got dark, but I reminded myself that an ambulance was on its way. All I had to do in the meantime was wait. Have a cup of tea. The room came back into focus.

There were other ways to heat water, I told myself. My gaze fell on the shiny silver kettle sitting on the stove top. I clawed my way towards it. Just like the cup, it was barely in reach. It was heavy in my hand, water sloshing as I tilted it. Full enough that I wouldn't have to try to figure out how to fill it. There, I told myself, everything was working out. I set the kettle back on the burner and turned on the igniter. The electronic click filled the room, a quickened metronome that was silenced by the low rumble of gas catching flame. I was too low to see how high the flame was, so I tried propping myself up to get a glimpse.

The room went black. I didn't pass out, exactly. I was still aware of my body existing in a place, I just had no connection to it. Sound, sight, it was all temporarily turned off. A short reboot. When I came to, my hand was propped against the top of the stove top. It took me a few moments to realize my fingers were laying in the flame of the burner.

I gasped, but didn't flinch away. The flame licked my skin, but I felt absolutely nothing. In fact, the same sensation that had been spreading over my surface was now numb in the tips of my fingers on my right hand. Relief shuddered through me. I pressed my hand further into the fire. It curled lovingly around my wrist, catching on the thick globs of white lotion. It spread, washing down my arm onto my shoulder and chest. I pulled my arm down and reached to touch the parts of me that were still bare. The room grew bright, so bright. An orange and yellow mosaic. A tear rolled down my face, evaporating into the air midway down my cheek. In the distance, I could hear a siren. I sighed, and leaned back against the wall that seemed to be made of light, sticking out my tongue to catch falling flames.

Meet the Authors

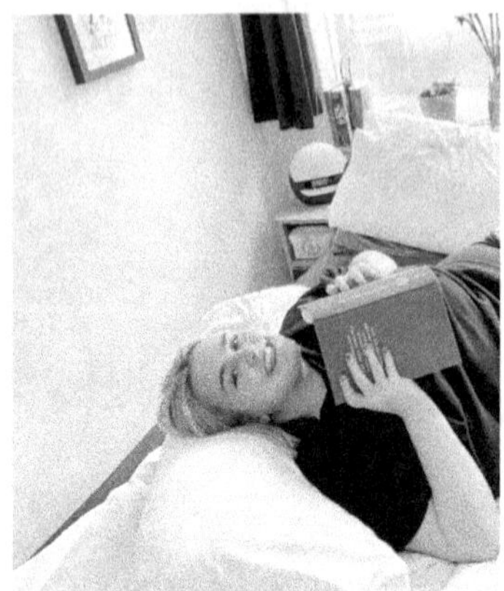

fig. 1 — Amber Donovan-Stevens

AMBER DONOVAN-STEVENS (fig. 1) is an English illustrator and writer based in London. She is drawn to horror that is particularly camp and, in recent years, has found a passion for slasher movies. Something in their predictability makes them immensely comforting. When she's not doing her day job in the big city, she illustrates for *Slow Burn Horror* and provides freelance illustration work for independent theatre and film companies.

Amber is interested in body horror and this is reflected in both her short story "Dosette Box" and in her illustrated work. Her current artistic project, *Memorphokuia*, explores extreme emotions manifested in the female form and draws inspiration from Japanese culture, and the Gothic, as well as artists Egon Schiele, Arthur Rackham, Dave Gibbons, and Ralph Steadman.

When she's not freaking out over African land snails, narrow spaces, or existential dread, she loves vibing out to animated horror films and makes playlists about horror films she will hopefully maybe someday write.

KATHRYN LEIGH (fig 2) is a writer and musician currently based in Cambridge, England.

They are drawn to the ambiguity of horror writing; it's a genre that allows and even requires you

fig. 2 — Kathryn Leigh

to pose questions without an answer. It's also a sandbox within which your characters can act as strange, depraved and disgusting as you like—always fun.

Kathryn is a fan of folk horror, the classic haunted house, and the inexplicable, almost-human-but-not-quite entities that occupy these spaces. In real life, sinkholes and vehicles falling into water are scary but thankfully not often encountered. They liked *The Wicker Man* (1973), *Starve Acre* by Andrew Michael Hurley, and are perpetually creeped out by the scribbles from Sarah Water's *The Little Stranger*.

You can hear them read "Kill Your Youngest" on the hallowed-histories.org podcast. They also write songs under the stage name "Thryn"—you can listen to them anywhere on the internet that music lives.

Shannon Lewis (fig 3) is a Mexican-American writer, editor, and general horror enthusiast based in Washington, USA. She is drawn to horror for the same reason she is drawn to magic realism, urban fantasy, and speculative fiction in general: a love of asking "what if?" A wide and varied genre, horror's unregimented structure and openness to all things weird lends itself to a creativity that she greatly appreciates.

She particularly likes folk horror that taps into primal fears, body horror that taps into abjection, "sleepover horror" (think *Saw, The Orphan*, the *Fear Street* trilogy), and of course slow burn horror that oozes off the page like wax down a candle. Personally, she is terrified of syringes and lumps, and is deeply mistrustful of fungi. Her favorite horror of all time includes *Mexican Gothic* by Silvia Moreno Garcia, "Nail" by Laura Hird, any short story by Tanarive Due, "The Yellow Wallpaper" by Charlotte Perkins Gilman, "Grease" by Junji Ito, *Beloved* by Toni Morrison (there's a ghost in it—it counts), *The Descent, Cam, The Babadook, Hereditary, Fire Walk with Me*, and the soundtrack to *Raw*.

Her thoughts on horror can be found across numerous blog posts on SlowBurnHorror.com (and in this anthology's intro).

fig. 4 — Harry Menear

Harry Menear (fig 4) is a writer and roleplaying game designer based in South Korea. He digs creeping dread, cosmic awfulness, and the shocking, unnatural

fig. 3 — Shannon Lewis

perversion of human flesh. He thinks horror is like picking at the scabbed-over bits inside our heads to let the baby spiders out, and the most honest way to look at who we are. But maybe he just likes wearing frilly black shirts and disappearing in clouds of smoke. He'll never tell.

His favorite horrifying things are, in no particular order: *Alien* by Ridley Scott, "The Haunter of the Dark" by H.P. Lovecraft, the 1959 murder of the Clutter Family, *Vecna Reborn* by Monte Cook, the shadow cast by someone standing in your blind spot, *The Witch* by Robert Eggers, and "Bela Lugosi's Dead" by Bauhaus. The thing that scares him most is the ceaseless devouring of human resources, potential, and blood by the insatiable maw of capitalism. Oh, and eels.

You can find his adventures—overwhelmingly designed for tabletop roleplaying games about dying horribly underground—at blackcitadelrpg.com and on DriveThruRPG.

Georgina Pearsall (fig 5) is a literature and creative writing graduate turned traitor currently studying to become an accountant. She is based in Essex and continues to write despite the confusion this causes her finance coworkers. She continues to study finance despite the confusion this causes her creative friends.

Georgina is primarily interested in any horror that explores creeping dread, with a particular fascination with ghosts. Her work follows her lifelong ambition to completely externalize her own struggle with anxiety until she can

fig. 5 — Georgina Pearsall

finally prove it was ghosts the entire time. Her biggest fears are the ocean, mutilation, and the feeling of being watched.

She loves the work of Shirley Jackson, Laura Hird, Susan Hill and any other horror by women she can get her hands on. She also strives to keep the Slow Burn collective abreast of developments in video game horror, even if she largely plays them with one hand over her eyes. She hopes one day to produce a piece of art one third as scary as Kitty Horrorshow's *Anatomy*.

Acknowledgements

To Amber, Kathryn, Georgie, and Harry: thank you. Thank you for writing wonderful, disturbing, lovely, awful short stories. This project was a team effort, with each of you not only acting as writers, but as editors, critics, readers, and hype-people. To Harry: thank you for your invaluable advice on Kickstarters and project campaigns. To Georgie: thank you for your editorial eye, for creating the Slow Burn style guide, and for bringing an accountancy brain to a lit student's attempts at budgeting. To Kathryn: thank you for your notes, for always being willing to indulge me in chats about horror, and for deciding for some ungodly reason to partner with me on yet another years-long writing project. Last but not least, thank you to Amber: for being my partner in *Slow Burn Horror* these last three years, for your eerie art, for creating a book cover that was lovelier than I could have dreamed it would be, for your dedication and patience, for bringing this anthology to life. Between the day we decided it would be kind of cool to publish a horror anthology to the day it was finally put to ink, we have been through a collective five moves, four career changes, three Halloweens, two weddings, one global pandemic, and a partridge in a pear tree. I would change nothing. To the four of you: I love you.

Thank you as well to everyone else who made this publication possible. To the 171 of you who pledged to our Kickstarter. To Nicole Robinson in particular, for being our largest donor (technically, you could say "patron") and a fervent supporter of all things horror. To MT Zimney for your crucial advice on self-publishing and for making the dream seem attainable. To Jayne at American Nightmare Candle Co. for bottling the smell of October to create a themed candle for this collection. To our beloved creative writing professor Jacob Huntley for agreeing for a second time to write an introduction to a horror project the five of us worked on. To Nat and Jackie for providing art for our Kickstarter extras and letting us be cool kids with actual merch. To Jackie as well for helping me record the Kickstarter video, for your advice on fonts, printing formats, and ICC profiles, and for basically formatting the entire anthology. Thank you to my parents and sister for their love and support. To Nikki for supplying me with a steady stream of tea (I'll admit in writing that you make a much better cuppa than I could ever hope). In fact, to all of our family and friends whose presence in our lives has created the people we are today, weirdos who think it's fun to write about creepy eggs and invasive moths: thank you.

And of course, thank you to Steve, for one day forgetting a carton of eggs in his bedroom after coming home from the shop, inadvertently kicking off this whole project.

Bibliography

Du Maurier, Daphne. *Echoes from the Macabre*. New York: First Avon Printing, 1978.

Due, Tananarive. "Free Jim's Mine." The Dark Magazine.

Due, Tananarive. "Like Daughter." Lightspeed. June, 2014.

Due, Tananarive. "Patient Zero." Lightspeed. August, 2010.

Fuentes, Carlos. *Aura*. New York: Farrar, Straus and Giroux, 1975.

Jackson, Shirley. *The Haunting of Hill House*. New York: Penguin Books, 2006.

Jackson, Shirley. *The Lottery and Other Stories*. New York: Farrar, Straus and Giroux, 2005.

Gilman, Charlotte Perkins. *The Yellow Wallpaper*. London: England: Virago Press, 1981.

Hill, Susan. *The Woman in Black*. New York: Vintage Books, 2014

Hird, Laura. *Nail and Other Stories*. Edinburgh: Rebel inc, 1997.

Hurley, Michael Andrew. *Starve Acre*. London: John Murray (Publishers), 2019.

Ito, Junji. *Shiver*. Tokyo: JI Ink, 2015.

LOVECRAFT, H. P. *Tales of the Cthulhu Mythos*. New York: Ballantine, 1998.

MORENO-GARCIA, Silvia. *Mexican Gothic*. London: Jo Fletcher Books, 2021.

MORRISON, Toni. *Beloved*. London: Vintage Classics, 2007.

NEERGAARD, E. *Carl Dreyer: A Film Director's Work*. London: BFI, 1950.

NICKEL, Philip J. "Horror and the idea of everyday life: On skeptical threats in psycho and the birds" In *The Philosophy of Horror*. New York: University Press of Kentucky, 2010. pp. 14--32.

POE, Edgar Allan. *The Illustrated Edgar Allan Poe*. London: Jupiter Books, 1976.

SHELLEY, Mary. *Frankenstein*. London: Penguin Classics, 2012.

STOKER, Bram. *Dracula*. Ware: Wordsworth Editions, 1993.

WATERS, Sarah. *The Little Stranger*. New York: Riverhead Books, 2018.